The waiter was back, looking apologetic. "I'm sorry," he said, handing Darcy the tray with the credit card. "We cannot accept your card. Would you like to pay cash?"

"Um, yes, we'll pay cash," Darcy said, her voice trembling ever so slightly. "Could you come back in a few minutes?"

The waiter melted oblingingly away, leaving Josh and Darcy facing one another across the table. "I don't understand," Darcy said. "My father's secretary pays my charge card bill out of the family account. Maybe he got behind mailing checks or something. . . . And I don't have any cash on me," she went on. "Josh, do you have any money?"

Josh's stomach gave a sickening lurch. Some nameless Jenner employee had screwed up, and now *he* was getting stuck with the bill. He swallowed, and got out his wallet. Luckily, it wasn't empty for once, but it was money he needed to pay rent.

"I'm sorry," Darcy said. "I had no idea this was going to happen —"

"Oh, c'mon," he said. "It's your own credit card. You mean you don't know if the bill's been paid or not?"

"No, I don't know if the bill's been paid or not," Darcy snapped back. "Because I don't pay it. I just —"

"You just spend it," Josh finished for her.

JUST FRIENDS

Jesse Maguire

IVY BOOKS • NEW YORK

Ivy Books
Published by Ballantine Books

Produced by Butterfield Press, Inc.
96 Morton Street
New York, New York 10014

Library of Congress Catalog Card Number 89-92450

ISBN   0-8041-0445-X

Manufactured in the United States of America

First Edition: May 1990

To the Core Four
and the kind of friendship that lasts forever

ONE

"Which do you think?" Mrs. Jenner asked, holding up two new dinner dresses still swathed in plastic wrap and studded with price tags.

Darcy shrugged, studying her own reflection in the antique mirror in her parents' bedroom. It was only about the millionth dinner party her mother had given — how could she possibly care if she wore cranberry or teal? "I don't know, Mom. They're both nice," Darcy said carelessly.

Mrs. Jenner's chin-length frosted hair bobbed as she tossed the dresses onto the bed. "You're sure a lot of help, honey," she said, her tone taking that quick swing, too familiar lately, from affectionate to irked.

"Sorry." Darcy lifted the silver hairbrush from her mother's dressing table, pressing its cool, scrolled back against her cheek. "Sorry I'm not Sarah," she added.

Darcy almost wished that for once her mother would say, "That makes two of us." But of course she didn't. A good parent never admitted she had a favorite, the picture-perfect oldest daughter who loved dressing up and playing the high-society part just like her mother; who graduated at the top of her exclusive prep school class and went on to equally exclusive Smith College just like her mother; who'd most likely "marry well" and live happily ever after just like her mother. . . .

"Darcy." Mrs. Jenner tilted her head, her grey eyes reproachful. "Did I mention your sister? Does this conversation have anything to do with her?"

"No." Darcy flipped the brush, stroking the bristles through her wavy brown hair. "Sorry again." She pretended to reconsider the question. *When all else fails, tell 'em what they want to hear.* She smiled at her mother and said, "Go with the teal."

"Thanks. I was leaning in that direction myself." Crossing the room, Mrs. Jenner took the hairbrush from Darcy's hand, replacing it carefully on the dressing table before planting a light kiss on her daughter's forehead.

Darcy slung an arm around her mother's shoulders, a quick squeeze, then hopped to her feet. "What time's this little get-together, anyway?"

"I'm expecting the Bennetts around seven. Why, are you going somewhere?" Mrs. Jenner asked, her narrowed eyes giving an edge to the casual question.

Darcy knew what was coming if she didn't exit the scene pronto. *Where? With whom? When will you be home?*

"I'm meeting some friends," she said, more evasion than explanation.

She didn't make it out the bedroom door in time. "What friends?"

Darcy stopped, turning to look her mother straight in the eye. "Friends from Norwell," she answered bluntly, emphasizing the last word because she knew any reference to her new high school gave her mother hives.

Mrs. Jenner's eyes narrowed further. "You've only been at Norwell a month. That seems awfully fast to have made such close friends that you have to rush off to see them again as soon as you get home from school."

"That bothers you, huh?" Darcy shook her head and smiled, even though to her mind the subject wasn't funny. "You sent me to Norwell as punishment, and now you're mad 'cause I actually *like* it?"

Reproach again. Mrs. Jenner crossed her arms over her chest, her expression speaking loud and clear: *This hurts me more than it hurts you. . . .*

Darcy waved a hand, deciding she wasn't about to stay for that guilt-inducing look. She cut out down the hallway, then down the wide staircase, taking the stairs two at a time. "I'm not exactly sure where I'm going and I don't know when I'll be back," she called airily over her shoulder, ducking out the front door before another question from her mother could lasso her back in.

The old silver Mercedes, her father's "everyday" car, was pulled up under the carport. Darcy sprinted toward it, her heels clattering on the flagstones. She had the spare set of keys — the loot was already stowed in the backseat. *I'm out of here!*

She put the car into first and pulled out of the long drive. Just minutes away from the house, and already she felt better. Boarding school had been stifling — the "Miss Manners" etiquette, the catty cliques, the whole idea that by the time you graduated you were "finished." What a feeling of freedom it was to leave Merton Hall last spring, forever. But living at home again, for the whole summer and now into the school year, had its own drawbacks. One common denominator: *rules.* "Didn't somebody say, though, rules were made to be broken?" Darcy wondered out loud as she spun the Mercedes onto High Ridge Road. Laughing at herself, she flipped the visor down against the low late afternoon sun. *Listen to me — Darcy Jenner, rebel without a cause. Yeah, right.*

Sometimes Darcy wondered just how her family got to the point where everything was so set, as if their way of life was an eleventh commandment carved in stone. By the book — that's how it was done, *had* been done for almost three centuries since the Jenners left the ancestral manor in England and cruised for new shores. Darcy had always considered herself a good girl, an obedient daughter. She'd been raised "right." As for rules, she'd only broken one significant one in her life. It *had* been a bit of a coup; she got herself kicked out of Merton Hall, after all. But that hardly constituted a life of crime.

Touching a button, Darcy sent all the car's windows purring down to half-mast. The Indian summer breeze stirred her hair and raised goose bumps on her bare arms. Ahead, a street light turned yellow. Pressing the gas pedal hard with one foot, Darcy whipped through the intersection, hanging a left onto Route 58 north just as the yellow deepened into stop-right-there red.

Darcy smiled again, ironically. Running red lights — that's about as far as she'd ever been willing to go in the direction of *bad*.

The lush wooded hills of her own neighborhood left behind, Darcy scanned the countryside now skimming past. Fields of tall toast-brown weeds, rusted-out road signs, the pock-marked structures of abandoned factories silhouetted against a yellow sky . . .

The badlands. Shivering, she shot the windows up a couple of inches. This part of town was like another world, *The Twilight Zone*. The Jenner estate, complete with a small staff of full-time "help," a manicured lawn, and an orderly English garden, might as well be on a separate planet, light-years away. Driving through the badlands, Darcy was conscious of the Mercedes's incongruity. It — she — didn't fit into this scene. It was like being on an old movie set, with a fan blowing her hair and fake scenery rolling by.

The bullet-riddled sign for Split River Bridge had alerted her to the turnoff. Bumping down the overgrown dirt road, Darcy glimpsed her destination ahead. The low, boarded-up brick building nestled next to the lethargic river and the long-disused railroad tracks — glowing like fire in the last rays of the sun, criss-crossing crazily, sending up sparks — Split River Station.

If the Merton girls could see me now! Steering the car out of sight around the far side of the station, Darcy bit back a giggle. She could practically smell Headmistress Bradstreet's generously applied Shalimar perfume, hear her tongue clicking sharply in disapproval. One of the cardinal *rules* of successful ladydom was keeping the "right" company and being seen in the "right" places. And Darcy knew Split River Station, and T.J. McAllister and Caroline Buchanan — the friends from Norwell High she'd mentioned to her mother — would hardly qualify.

Darcy had met T.J. on her first day at Ernest Norwell High, the day Jenner forefathers and foremothers rolled over in their graves because one of their own had set foot inside a *public* school. Which was something Darcy was happy enough to do, having had her fill of prep-school pretensions. Her parents abhorred the school but resorted to it as a disciplinary measure after the Merton escapade. T.J. was new, too, an out-of-towner. Despite his newness, though, or rather because of it, T.J. had been the one to discover probably the best hideout in Redmond, Pennsylvania. A grown-up's fort, a treehouse for teenagers.

A couple of bikes leaned haphazardly against the station's worn stone steps. Clutching two bulging grocery bags, Darcy stepped carefully toward the building, grimacing as her leather flats filmed over with soot and dust. She reached the space where a couple of loose boards and a broken window permitted access to the deserted railway station. Inside she heard rock music and voices. *Must be Caro and T.J.*

"Ready or not, here I come!" Darcy called cheerfully. "And this is going to be a fashionable entrance, for sure, in a miniskirt. T.J., I'll have to request that you avert your eyes!"

"Whoa, hold it!" T.J.'s green eyes looked up at Darcy from the dim light inside. "Station renovation stage two includes sealing the windows against those nasty drafts that cause the common cold and *un*-sealing the door so we can come and go like human beings instead of foraging squirrels!"

T.J. disappeared from the window. Darcy heard a creaking of hinges to her left, and the station's heavy wooden door actually swung open. At the top of the stairs, T.J. bowed low.

"Trick or treat," said Darcy.

"Welcome to Castle Dracula," T.J. said in his suavest blood-sucking voice.

The thick oak door slammed shut behind them. "Stage two, huh?" Darcy looked around the small but high-ceilinged station. The moldy rolled-up carpet was gone, and some furnishings of dubious origin had taken its place. Maybe it looked a little cleaner? It'd been so filthy before it was hard to tell. "What was stage one?" she asked.

"*What* was stage *one*?" Caroline Buchanan repeated, her husky voice colored with laughter. "Stage one was mops and brooms and bucket after bucket of some kind of pine-scented cleaner and a terminal case of dishpan hands!"

"It wasn't *that* bad," T.J. protested, ruffling a hand through Caroline's silvery-brown hair. "I only lost three layers of skin myself."

Turning aside to dump the bags onto a moth-eaten green velveteen sofa, Darcy swallowed a sudden wave of shyness. Even though she'd been sharing lots of time and space and conversation with them of late, T.J. and Caro were still so *new*. At least, new to *her*. Different from her other friends, her childhood pal Sue Rhiner and the wealthy, well-bred girls and guys from Merton Hall and its "brother" prep school, Kingsford.

T.J. rubbed his hands together and licked his lips greedily. "What'dya bring, Darce, old sport?"

"Well, let's see." Darcy reached into a bag, glad to have something to do. "A pair of brass candlesticks." She dug down again. "Another pair of brass candlesticks." Her smile was apologetic. "I'm not kidding, we have a basement full of these things. Wedding gifts my parents never used in twenty-five years," she hurried to add in explanation, in case it sounded like she was boasting about her family's abundance of worldly goods.

T.J. helped Darcy unload. "And a box of fancy candles, natch," he observed.

Caroline smiled that soft sideways smile, her green eyes crinkling at T.J. "I don't know . . . candles? Could create a romantic atmosphere. *Might* be dangerous, hmm, McAllister?"

It would have been hard to miss the look that passed between the two of them. Darcy didn't. *What's* really *going on there?* she wondered for at least the fiftieth time. She and Caro had become friends, but they still weren't *close*. Caroline was deeply private and very independent; Darcy had a feeling she didn't let many people get near. Only T.J., and even that didn't seem to be a conventional relationship.

"*And* a crocheted afghan *and* a bunch of posters," continued T.J. without missing a beat. Unrolling a poster with a snap, he hooted. "Panda bears!"

"Be merciful," pleaded Darcy. "They're off the walls of my old room at Merton. The best I could do on short notice."

"Fear not. On *these* walls, anything goes. Endangered animals and Hollywood hunks are fine by me. You, Caro?"

Caroline winked slyly at Darcy. "*I'm* kind of growing attached to all the spray-painted four-letter words."

T.J. made a grab for her, but Caroline slipped through his fingers, laughing. "Naughty girl," he reprimanded.

Naughty girl . . . Another difference between us. Caroline Buchanan had a "reputation." That was about all Darcy had known about her until she talked with Caro herself and found out she might be "fast," but she was also fair. Fair, and genuinely kind, a far cry from Norwell's other "cool" girls like Holly Vickers and the Rat Pack. Caroline had been willing to give Darcy a chance, see beyond *her* reputation as a snobby prep.

T.J. and Caroline had both accepted Darcy. It was natural, maybe. Caro the lone wolf, T.J. the new boy at odds with the old boys from day one, Darcy an exile from the land of boarding schools and debutante balls. Maybe it was natural they'd found each other — and the station.

As Caroline and T.J. argued about what tape to blast next from the boombox, Darcy curled up on the couch and looked around with thoughtful eyes. Split River Station had been officially abandoned for decades, but it was easy to see it'd never been lonely. Countless hoboes and kids had autographed the walls using whatever was handy, penknives, spray paint, or nail polish. The night of the Kick-off Dance was the first time T.J. had shown Darcy and Caro the station. A hideaway, he'd called it. A place where the only rule was there were no rules, Caro had added.

That night the station hadn't exactly looked like the lobby of the Plaza Hotel, being buried under about a hundred years of grime and a hundred generations of spiders' webs. Spotless it would never be, but now that she looked a little closer, Darcy could see that T.J. and Caro had definitely made a dent in the dirt. With the sofa, three tattered summer lounge chairs, a pair of hurricane lamps, and a battery-operated space heater, it was actually verging on "cozy." T.J. had even polished the bars of the old wrought-iron ticket booth.

"You know, I *loathe* housework," Caro mused, obviously on the same wavelength as Darcy. "I'd jog naked down Main Street before I'd voluntarily vacuum or mop at my dad's apartment. But here . . . "

T.J. dropped onto one of the lounge chairs, causing a few more of the plastic straps to give out. "It's different," he said simply.

Caroline, standing by the broken window, turned her face away. "Yeah."

Darcy was watching T.J. His eyes were on Caro's back and it looked to Darcy like he was ready to launch out of the lounge guided-missile fashion. But he must have read something in the stiff attitude of Caro's shoulders that told him to stay put.

T.J. would do anything to make Caro happy, Darcy marveled silently. *He knows she's miserable at her own house so he dreamed this up.* It made sense. It could work. Maybe they all needed it, for the freedom if nothing else. Caro, T.J., her, Josh — especially Josh . . .

"Josh." Darcy jumped, afraid she'd somehow spoken her thoughts out loud. But it was Caroline, at the window. "Damn, when he rides that bike he flies. Like something's *chasing* him."

T.J. sprang from his seat, reached the door in two strides, and bellowed a hearty greeting, "Hickham, my man! Welcome to McAllister's Pleasure Palace and Hotdog Hut."

Through the doorway Darcy glimpsed Josh's trail bike, tossed on its side with its wheels still spinning. And Josh, panting, his longish brown hair swept back from his handsome, angular face and damp at the temples from exertion.

Darcy shook her head, thinking that Josh Hickham had to be one of the best-looking guys in the entire state, and he didn't even know it. Josh always seemed to have other things on his mind.

"Hey, Josh!" Caroline flashed him a warm smile.

"Hey," Darcy echoed, hoping it wasn't obvious to everybody she was blushing slightly.

"He reaches into his bag of tricks and pulls out . . . a dart board! *Excellent!*" T.J. flourished the prize that Josh had carried wrapped in a plastic trash bag.

Josh drew a smaller bundle from the pocket of his faded denim jacket. "And what goes better with a dart board than darts?" He half smiled, sort of unsure. Darcy laughed and then felt suddenly lightheaded when, meeting her eyes, Josh's smile widened. Because he didn't smile all that much. Too often, Darcy thought, Josh's face looked tense and tight. It was home that was the problem for him, too, she gathered, same as for Caroline, whose mother had split years earlier leaving Caro to be raised by a boozing father. From the sound of it, Josh had a stepmother so nasty she made Cinderella's look sweet. Watching T.J. and Josh hang a few posters, Darcy felt ashamed all of a sudden. She'd been feeling crowded at home earlier, but how could she imagine she had anything to complain about compared to her friends? She lived in a beautiful house with two parents who loved her — in their own way.

It seemed like Josh had just breezed in and then he was checking his watch. He pivoted toward the door with a thin nervous movement. "Can't stay. Got here so late 'cause the Witch made me baby-sit for the midget monsters," he explained, referring distastefully to his stepmother and younger half-siblings. "I've got to be at Jake's in fifteen minutes."

They all understood about Josh's hectic double life — working nights at Jake's burger stand so he could pay the rent his stepmother charged him. T.J. clapped Josh on the shoulder. "Thanks for making the heroic effort."

Josh shrugged. "We needed stuff for the wall, right?"

"Any basic decorative artifacts are welcome. . . . "

Josh looked guilty. He put a hand on the doorknob, his eyes lowered. "I really gotta make tracks." Outside the dusk sky had clouded to purple and the air pushing through the door was cold. "But I'll be around to toss some darts," he promised.

"You know the way," T.J. said easily.

"Wait!" Darcy spoke up. If it was almost six o'clock, it was time for her to head out as well. "Josh, I'll give you a ride," she offered.

"*You* working at Jake's, *too*?"

Darcy laughed at T.J.'s raised eyebrows. "No." She adopted a hoity-toity tone, nose in the air. "A dinner party with some business associates of my father's, don't you know. The guests will be arriving any minute and I haven't even decided what gown to wear."

"See you guys tomorrow in homeroom, then," called Caro by way of good-bye. "At least it'll be bearable — T. G. I. F. !"

The Mercedes gleamed lavender in the sharp autumn twilight. As Darcy unlatched the trunk and Josh gingerly stowed his bike they were both silent. She tried not to notice or be bothered by the contrast, but it was there, inescapable. Her fancy car — his beat-up bike. She was heading home to a meal prepared by a hired cook — he had to work at a greasy take-out joint to make money to pay the rent. Darcy got that *Twilight Zone*, light-years-away feeling again. *You Tarzan, me Jane. But we live in different jungles . . .*

Josh was awkward handling the bike, as if he were afraid to mar the Mercedes's silver paint with the tiniest scratch. In the passenger seat, though, awkwardness gave way to exhaustion. He sank back, stretching his legs out full length. "Thanks, Darcy," he breathed. "This is the first chance all day I've had to relax."

"No problem." Making a U-turn, Darcy sent the Mercedes's headlights skittering in a bright arc across the dry, ghostly grass.

She opened her mouth again to say something light and witty, something to show Josh she understood how it was with his family and all, but without making a big deal about it. Something, anything, just to reach across the gulf that separated them.

Casting a glance sideways, Darcy swallowed the remark. Josh had shut his eyes — shut her out, shut out the world.

"A tiger in a too-small cage at the zoo, that's what you make me think of," T.J. observed.

Caroline turned to face him, the heel of her boot squeaking on the wood floor. "A tiger in a too-small cage . . . " That was exactly how she felt. Trust T.J. to get right inside her and put her feelings into words.

She smiled. "Am I pacing that bad?"

T.J. was holding Josh's dart board up to the station's north wall. "Let's just say the word 'restless' comes to mind," he answered, the nails clenched between his teeth making him sound like Humphrey Bogart.

Making a conscious effort to unwind, Caro lay down on the velveteen sofa, planting her boots unceremoniously on one of the threadbare arms. There was a lot of noise as T.J. hammered the dart board into place, but she knew he was still listening, still tuned to her. "I've just been getting kind of like, *crazy*, you know? With my car in the shop," she explained to the raftered ceiling. The '65 Mustang had needed major repairs after the night she'd used it to run interference between Shet Vickers's gang and Leon Fiero.

My car was my legs, Caro continued, silently. *And I still need to run . . .*

T.J. threw a glance at her, his green eyes flickering with understanding. A hot shivery feeling chased itself in a quick circle inside Caro's stomach. Talk about crazy, what was *really* crazy was with T.J. the way sometimes she didn't even have to *talk*.

He'd done it the first day, or rather dawn, he met her. She'd found him walking along the side of the road in mud-caked socks after a night of initiation into Who's Who and What's What in Redmond, starting with a rough-up courtesy of Shet Vickers, that punk. But even in a definitely awkward situation, T.J. McAllister hadn't been at a disadvantage. Five, six in the morning and that mind of his, those eyes of his, were relentless. He figured things, and people, out fast.

"Biking," T.J. said, tossing an experimental dart.

Caro groaned. "Don't start."

"I'm starting and I won't stop until you fully appreciate the joys of bike riding!" He threw another dart, this time with a fancy around-the-back maneuver. "The wind in your face, the physical challenge, feeling like you're one with the open road . . ."

"*Yawn*," declared Caroline, but smiling in response

to T.J.'s teasing grin. "No power, no *noise*. Give me a car any day if you really want to get places."

"Move those big ol' feet." T.J. lifted Caro's legs, pushed her affectionately aside, and sat down next to her.

Damn, Caro thought, pretending to be interested in a nicked spot on her left boot. *If T.J. and I are "just friends," then why do I get goose bumps whenever he touches me?* "The place is lookin' great," she commented, focusing now on the dart board.

"None too shabby for just a couple afternoons' work," agreed T.J. "A much more comfortable place to crash than it was the first night I hid out with Woofer, that's for sure."

Alison Laurel's twelve-year-old brother had traded T.J. "rights" to the abandoned station in exchange for martial-arts lessons. "Do you grant Woofer visiting privileges at least?" Caro asked, nudging T.J.'s half-zipped backpack with one toe.

"Any time. Plus we're still meeting here for our self-defense lessons, Saturdays, six a.m. sharp."

"Isn't that a little early?"

"I'm used to it." T.J. turned to look at her. His arm was stretched along the back of the sofa and now his fingers brushed against her hair. So lightly, and then the hand slipped away again. But to Caro that small gesture said more than a whole book full of words.

Quickly, she leaned forward, her hair swinging across her face, hiding it. She poked in the backpack. "Food! Where'd this come from?"

"Cupboards at home. Don't tell my mom — I filched it."

"Peanut butter, a loaf of bread, chips, trail mix — T.J., you pig." Caro pushed her hair back and laughed at him. "You eat all that now, it'll spoil your appetite for dinner. Then your mom will *really* be pissed."

"Oh, it's not necessarily for immediate consumption," he explained. "Just thought I'd leave it around here. Emergency munching material, you know."

I know. Josh, Caroline guessed. Josh whose stepmother made him pay rent. Josh who never had any lunch at school and was so damn skinny, it was a miracle that when he got up speed on his bike he didn't just take off into the air like the Flying Nun.

It was only about the millionth thing like this T.J. had done since she'd met him. Always looking out for people, caring about them, and trying to help in a way they'd never notice. A warm, grateful feeling flooded Caroline's body right to her fingertips. T.J. was smiling, knowing he'd been found out. "Oh, McAllister, *you!*"

Without thinking, Caro reached out to hug him. She meant the hug to be quick. A *friendly* hug, a thanks for being such a great guy hug. But when T.J.'s arms wrapped around her, reciprocating, she caught her breath at a memory so sharp it almost hurt.

Driving rain . . . lightning so wild it was like fireworks . . . the station dark and musty, before . . . The night of the Kick-off Dance, the night she'd said goodbye to Leon Fiero, forever. T.J. and her, on the moldy rolled-up carpet. It was funny she'd be attracted to skinny ol' T.J. Sure, he was good-looking, but other than that he wasn't anything like the guys she usually went out with. Still, that kiss . . . it had torn her in two. Caroline had never felt such good, happy love.

As for T.J. . . . he said it was because he wanted her so much, cared for her so much, that he wouldn't go any further. There had to be more than sex between them. They'd be friends first. *First.* He was the first guy she'd come across who didn't want to jump in the *sack* first. The concept "friendship" had not been an operative part of most guys' relationships; but then it hadn't exactly been priority one with her, either.

Now T.J.'s face was warm against her hair. *It'd be so easy to turn my head just a couple of inches,* Caro thought. She knew T.J. was thinking the same thing. *Our lips would touch — it'd just happen.*

She pulled back slightly to rest her forehead against his chest. Her laugh was low and vibrant. "T.J. McAllister," she murmured into his sweater, "if I didn't know better, I'd think I — I think I'm not going to say what I was just going to say!"

She lifted her head and met T.J.'s eyes. They told her he knew exactly what she was going to say — and exactly why she didn't say it.

TWO

"Yo, braindead!" For a second, Josh Hickham's fingers froze on the open door of his locker and his back stiffened blindly. He could swear he felt Shet Vickers's gunmetal-grey eyes boring through his shoulderblades, exposing his unworthy heart.

Slam. The locker door latched, quivering. Relaxed, Josh turned slowly. The pleasant endearment had been Shet's but the weasely voice wasn't, not by a long shot.

"Hughes, you putz," Josh said amiably. *How's the butt-kissing business?* he almost added. But it wasn't that long since he'd been kissing butt as bad as Art, trying to fit in with the cool guys. King Cool Leon Fiero and Shet, the Crown Prince of Cool who wanted to be king.

Art Hughes fell into step beside Josh. They pushed down the hallway, jostling with the other students.

"You missed another band practice," Art said. "Matt's gonna be rustlin' up another roadie if you don't show today."

"Maybe he ought to do that," Josh advised. "Maybe I won't be showing."

"Aw, ya got somethin' better to do?" Art's sneer was classic. "You and Mr. Poser McAllister gonna sell some Girl Scout cookies?"

Josh took a hard elbow in his left side. When he turned to shoot a dirty look at the elbow's owner, Trissa Lemek snapped her gum in his face and then gave him a sugary, lash-fluttering smile. Josh laughed. Just like Art wasn't so tough since Shet and Leon had moved out of town, Trissa wasn't quite the rat she'd been when she had Shet's twin sister Holly to back her up.

"Got somethin' better to do?" Art asked again.

"Yep. Granite Action'll have to rock 'n' roll without me."

"You had your chance," Art intoned in what was supposed to be a threatening manner. Josh couldn't help it; instead of shaking in his shoes the way Art clearly thought he should, he was actually enjoying this.

"Have a riot sweating for Matt's band," Josh said with a grin. He veered off toward English class, ditching Art.

He felt light, flowing with the noisy crowd toward Room 113. Art was funny, he thought, a real cartoon character. Talking tough, not even realizing that without Shet to give them a motive to be mean, the rest of the gang was just a bunch of guys who hung out together.

I got the easy way out, Josh reflected, his eye caught by a flash of scarlet — a girl in a bright red leather micromini hanging on the arm of some punk trying to look like Sting. *I'm off the hook. I don't have to pretend anymore, give up my whole personality like Art did so people will think I'm cool.* He was on his own again and it felt good. Or rather, he'd made some *real* friends. When he was with T.J., Josh didn't have to put on an act, maybe because it hadn't taken T.J. long to discover Josh would rather be drawing than kowtowing to Shet and company.

A workroom . . . T.J. had said Split River Station, once it was fixed up a bit, could be a workroom, some place where Josh could sketch without worrying about his stepmother's snide remarks or other kids' ridicule. *So why'd I wimp out last night, bring that stupid dart board instead some of my drawings?* he wondered, mad at himself for being such a coward. Next time — next time he stopped by the station he'd bring some art supplies and stuff. . . .

A nightmare of impossible colors assaulted Josh's right eye as he cut through the lobby, his English class being two doors down the south wing. He had to look — he always looked every time he passed it, even though it made him want to puke, aesthetically speaking. The famous Ernest Norwell High mural, a couple dozen 1930's whitebread superkids marching in single file, the girls with rosy cheeks and books clutched demurely to their chests and the boys in midget businessman suits and ties.

No kids ever looked like that, not in a million years.

They hung weirdly in space, the lighting all wrong. Whoever painted it didn't know the first thing about art, or *life*, that's for sure.

Josh caught sight of a familiar figure a couple of bodies ahead of him. The wavy ash-brown hair was neatly brushed as always, falling in perfect, untouchable strands across her cashmere shoulders. *She* could almost be a mural kid come to life and updated for the nineties. "Darcy, hey, wait up!" Josh called.

Darcy turned, her hair swinging in a glossy arc like some kind of shampoo commercial. "Hey, yourself," she responded, holding her books up against her chest and looking more than ever like she'd stepped out of the somewhere-over-the-rainbow picture on the wall. "What class do you have now?"

"English." Josh and Darcy were now squeezed against a row of lockers, relatively safe from the trampling mainstream. "What am I making you late for?"

"Just study hall," Darcy said. "Gossip hall, I mean. Caro has it, too. Mr. Silver's the monitor, but he's too busy counting the minutes till he can cut loose and light a cigarette to care how loud we talk."

"You guys should just walk out," Josh suggested glibly.

"Hmm . . . hit the courts with Caro and study up on our tennis game for a change of pace," Darcy agreed.

"You're gonna be late anyway," Josh predicted, casing the thinning crowd in the hall. He was kind of glad they didn't have much time to talk, even though he'd been the one to flag her down. He liked Darcy, but he didn't always know how to act when he was around her.

Darcy waved a hand, an imperious Princess Diana-type gesture. Josh pictured her using it with the Jenner servants, a magic wand for directing any situation. "I'll just tell Silver I was out back finishing a Salem," she joked. "Get his mouth watering and distract him. See you at lunch maybe?"

Josh nodded. They were at the door of his English class; Darcy still had a whole corridor to traverse. "Later, Darce."

Mouth watering . . . speaking of which . . . English passed, chemistry, American History, and then Josh was swimming down the hallway again, this time toward the cafeteria with Caroline and T.J.

Lunch. Josh knew he was the only kid in the school who dreaded lunch period. Sure, it was okay hanging out, talking loud, being out from behind a desk for an hour. But for somebody who'd only snatched a bite for breakfast and wouldn't taste another till he reported for work at the burger stand, the cafeteria smells and the sight of hundreds of people chowing down was torture. A torture to which Josh was pretty well accustomed, however. He *could* spring for an occasional lunch with what was left over from his pay after he shelled out the month's rent to the Witch, but then there'd be nothing to buy pens and paper with.

Caroline was craning her neck. "I see Mouse and Darce," she announced, pleased.

The three struck a course through the jam-packed

room. Josh had often thought the cafeteria was like some kind of map. Different territories were charted out as clearly as if there were lines painted on the linoleum floor. Juniors here, seniors there, *cool* seniors there, the Smart Set in one corner, jocks milling in another.

They reached theater arts country, where Darcy was sitting with Alison Laurel and a bunch of kids Josh recognized from the arty creative band Alison sang with — Corrie and his spectacularly thick glasses, plump Liz who had a voice like an opera diva, Noah, and Harrison.

"Welcome!" Alison greeted them in her sweet singer's voice. If T.J. hadn't propelled him into a chair, Josh might have stood there for the rest of lunch, staring like a geek. It was just that even when she wasn't singing, Alison's voice was like music. Hearing her, seeing her, Josh remembered the afternoon the gang had spent at the Salvation Army, and Alison creating a magical costume from eclectic cast-offs. Alison, who saw colors the way he did.

Caro started quizzing Darcy about the dinner party at her house the night before while T.J. rapped with Harrison about jazz piano techniques. Josh found himself next to Alison, his chair practically touching hers, the table was that crowded. He looked down into her eyes, which were as warm and dark and soft as cattails.

"Congratulations," Josh said. "About the Kick-off Dance."

Alison's band had been one of two winners at the band competition, along with Granite Action.

"Thanks!" Her smile was radiant. "Matt's band will play the homecoming dance and we'll do the Christmas one. We even get paid! Only thing, Corrie's turned into a real slave driver. He's turning his brain inside out writing songs *and* he's got us practicing like maniacs."

From Alison's other side, Noah patted her hand. "Poor little Mouse," he said in a brotherly tone.

Alison laughed and Josh, feeling suddenly self-conscious, wished he had a sandwich, even a carton of milk — something to look at besides Alison. It wasn't long ago he'd have sat at just about any other table in the cafeteria rather than squeeze himself between two girls as gorgeous as Alison Laurel and Caroline Buchanan. Girls didn't scare him — he wasn't that backward. But they mystified him and made him uncomfortable, the way they flirted on any excuse. Caroline and Darcy and Alison were different, though, probably, Josh thought, because he considered them friends, not just girls. Well, that wasn't entirely true. Alison made his head swim slightly.

"You were the best. The best band," Josh said quickly, realizing he'd been gawking at Alison for about a month.

Alison spooned into her yogurt. "You really think so?" she asked.

"Sure. I mean, you were *original*. Not the songs, maybe, but your interpretation of them. Your music was alive."

She nodded. "It *feels* alive when we play together. I love it — it's the best high there is."

Josh knew what Alison was talking about. Alive, high, that was the way his art made *him* feel. But as for sharing it the way Alison did, up on stage in front of the whole world, he didn't find that easy at all. But Alison understood. He could explain himself to her.

"Listening to your band," he began shyly, "I didn't just *hear* the music, d'you know what I mean? It's like sometimes when I see something I want to draw. It's not just the colors and shapes that grab me, it's some kind of spirit."

Josh looked down at his hands lying on the table, wishing he could rewind and erase the last fifteen seconds of the tape. How stupid had that sounded? By now Alison was probably convinced that he was a total dork.

No she wasn't. "You draw, Josh? I should've guessed. You *talk* like an artist, the way you express things."

Alison's interested smile made the knot of embarrassment and insecurity in Josh's stomach melt. *But don't start blabbering*, he warned himself. *Don't scare her off by laying seventeen years of frustrated artistic aspiration on her all at once!* Maybe he'd said enough for now. Maybe it was time to switch back to a more neutral channel. Say something like, what are you doing for the rest of your life?

Corrie's voice cut in on Josh's thoughts. "Chug that yogurt, Al. Rehearsal in five minutes."

Alison turned to face him and Josh looked around, having half forgotten he and Alison weren't alone at the table. Darcy's wide-set cornflower-blue eyes were fixed on him with an odd, unreadable expression. She'd probably heard him talking about art and was thinking he was a geek. Or she was speculating about his lack of lunch. To Darcy, whose brown paper bag was filled with gourmet delicacies prepared by the Jenners' personal chef, Josh must be a quaint sociological case study. He reddened self-consciously.

"You just don't have the right appreciation for Superman," T.J. was saying to Caroline.

"I appreciate Superman plenty," Caroline retorted with a provocative smile. "I like a guy in tight pants, if he's got a hot bod that is."

T.J. rolled his eyes. "Wrong, Miss Buchanan. Superman is a work of art and intellect, not a male exotic dancer. Now, Lois — her I wouldn't mind seeing in a leotard. . . ."

Tuning in to T.J. and Caro, Josh tuned out his thoughts about Darcy and Alison and lunch and art. Comic books were safer ground, a make-believe world where you could always tell the good guys from the bad.

"Twelve-ten High Ridge, please," Darcy instructed the taxi driver.

After the last bell she'd strolled a discreet distance from the school building toward the busier stretch of Main Street, before hailing a cab. Being seen would be too humiliating. It would confirm everybody's theory that she was a spoiled-rotten rich kid.

The truth was, though, Darcy couldn't bear the

school bus. She'd tried it. Been squashed in a seat with a large guy in a greasy jeans jacket practically sitting on her lap. Had putrid clove cigarette smoke blown into her hair by the kid behind her. Opened the window to get some air and then couldn't get it shut again when it started raining. Of course, nobody offered to help, even the big guy who probably could've closed it with his pinky. Naturally she got soaked.

In the morning, the bus wasn't so bad. Kids were still half asleep, too drowsy to bicker or smoke. But Darcy had sworn to herself *never again* in the afternoon. *So I* am *spoiled rotten once every day at two-thirty*, she thought, sliding across the slippery vinyl seat as the driver made a sharp turn. *So sue me!*

Slim white trunks of birch trees and a wash of golden leaves passed in a blur by the window as the cab headed east into the the hills. A flash of diamonds — river falls. Another half mile of sprawling houses on broad lawns behind forbidding walls and she'd be home.

The fresh beauty of the autumn afternoon barely registered on Darcy. More vivid than the birches and the bubbling river was the picture of Josh agog over Alison at lunch. Well, maybe not *agog*. He wasn't actually drooling, and Alison hadn't seemed to notice anything out of the ordinary. But Darcy had spent enough time with Josh to recognize atypical behavior. With any other guy, it'd be a safe bet he had a crush.

Am I disappointed? Darcy asked herself. *Sure, a little. I wouldn't mind too much if Josh stared at me that way.* Half the time, Josh didn't look at her at all when they talked. He looked down, to the sides, over her head. . . .

"This it?" the driver asked, breaking into her thoughts.

"Yes, on the left."

The cab driver swung into the Jenner driveway, past the grey stone gateposts. A quarter mile exactly, and he stopped under the carport. Darcy felt around in her shoulder bag for her wallet. She handed up a couple of bills. "Thanks a lot."

There were two extra cars parked in the drive this afternoon. Somebody's new hunter-green BMW, and her grandfather's Rolls.

Darcy smiled. In the summer and fall Grandpa Jenner spent most of his time out at his second home on the Delaware shore. He hadn't visited them since school started and she missed him, more than ever lately since he was the only person who didn't make her feel rotten for getting kicked out of Merton and disgracing the family name. Plus Grandpa Jenner was associated with extravagant gifts, sort of like Santa Claus. Darcy knew she shouldn't be greedy, but she couldn't help it. *What'd he bring me this time?* she wondered. Last time it was an alligator-skin wallet, and the time before that a CD player she'd been wanting.

She stepped into the parquet-floored front hall. There he was, a thin but erect man with a surprisingly thick thatch of pure white hair.

"Darcy, sugar!"

"Grandpa! It's about time you showed up here!"

"Think I'd forget about my little girl?"

A big bear hug and then Grandpa Jenner stepped back to look at her. "She doesn't *look* like a public-school girl," he announced loudly for the benefit of her parents in the west front parlor.

"Oh, Grandpa, it's not so bad," Darcy lectured. "Teachers and homework like any other kind of school."

"It's the *atmosphere*, dear," he said sternly, but his tanned, lined face crinkled in a smile. "I don't blame you for sowing a few wild oats at your age," he added in a conspiratorial whisper. "Wish I was sixteen again!"

Darcy gave him a playful shove. "Oh, c'mon, Grandpa. Don't play old with me! You know you're as much of a kid as I am."

They entered the parlor, Grandpa Jenner holding Darcy's arm hooked in his. "Hi, Mom. Hi, Dad," she said.

Her mother stood poised by the marble-topped bar, a crystal decanter of sherry in her hand. "Honey, tell me you didn't go to school dressed like *that*."

Darcy looked down at herself. Jeans with a rip in one knee and a pastel cashmere cardigan buttoned up over nothing. "Mom, I don't go to Merton anymore," she said, unable to prevent a note of antagonism from creeping in.

Her mother's gaze was coolly disapproving. "Just because the girls at Norwell dress like tramps doesn't mean you have to emulate them. You're still — "

"I know, I know. A *Jenner*." Darcy laughed, pretending that her mother's critical remarks didn't sting. "Don't worry. I haven't forgotten!"

"I think she looks charming," Grandpa Jenner interjected diplomatically. "Cute as a button. I'm partial to these new casual styles myself."

"Perrier, darling?" Mrs. Jenner reached for a glass, changing the topic abruptly.

"Sure, thanks," Darcy said, accepting the peace offering. She planted a kiss on top of her father's balding head, then drifted toward the bow window facing the side lawn. That current was in the air again, the same tense electricity she felt last time her grandfather came. Had they been talking about her?

"So you took our portfolio away from Sturgis and Wieland?" Grandpa Jenner asked Darcy's father. She listened curiously.

"Those market losses were their fault," her father said, sounding defensive, Darcy thought. "I'll manage the investments myself from here on if I can't find a firm that doesn't treat their clients' funds like Monopoly money."

There was a loud clink of glass on glass. Darcy jumped. Her mother had placed a Perrier on the coffee table.

The sound seemed to have acted as a signal to Grandpa Jenner as well. "We'll continue our conversation in the study after we've heard from Darcy about her day at school," he announced matter-of-factly.

Darcy's father nodded in assent, and Darcy realized that even though her grandfather was rarely around, he was still the undisputed head of the family — and that had to be hard on her father.

"Come here, missy," her grandfather said, trying to sound stern.

Obediently, Darcy took a seat next to him on the brocade divan.

"Are you getting all A's in your classes?"

"Too soon to say. But I'll send you a copy of my report card when it comes, shall I?" she teased.

"Smart alec. I'm just making certain because — " Grandpa Jenner paused. Underneath his bushy white eyebrows, his blue eyes twinkled.

"Because why?" she prompted, guessing it was gift time.

"Because only a straight-A student deserves a brand-new . . . "

Remembering the strange BMW in the driveway, Darcy leapt to her feet with a squeal. Grandpa Jenner nodded at the front window, through which the dark sleek car was visible. "To cheer you up, after that business at Merton. To get you to school in style, dear."

In five seconds flat Darcy was out the door and running a hand admiringly over the hood of the car. "It's gorgeous," she murmured. "Is it really mine?"

"Surprised?" Her grandfather stood in the doorway, enjoying her reaction. Darcy sprang to give him a grateful hug. "Admit it, sugar. You've been expecting it since your sixteenth birthday."

"Well . . . " Darcy grinned.

He held out the keys. "Take it for a spin, why don't you. While I chat for a while longer with your mom and dad."

A *spin* . . . Darcy couldn't wait to get her hands on

the steering wheel. Her very first drive was too important not to share, though. She hesitated, her hand suspended over the phone in the hall. Sue Rhiner? She and Sue had shared every single joy and toy since babyhood. But Sue wouldn't exactly be thrilled over a new BMW — she'd been driving her own Jag since April.

Caro! Darcy dialed impatiently. After an endless five rings Caroline answered, and Darcy jingled the keys next to the mouthpiece so her friend could hear. "Guess what, Buchanan. I — *we've* — got wheels!"

THREE

Caroline gave a long, low whistle. "God, Darcy, when you said a new *car* I thought *Chevy!*"

Gingerly placing herself on the butter-soft leather seat, Caro caught Darcy's blush. "Oh, I — I, well . . . " Darcy stammered. "My grandfather — kind of extravagant — spoils me . . . "

Caro cut her off with a slam of the car door and a grin. "Don't apologize, you idiot. I, for one, wouldn't look a gift BMW in the mouth or under the hood or wherever. You got it, flaunt it, I always say!"

Starting the engine, Darcy looked relieved by her friend's easy acceptance.

There's no point making a fuss, Caroline thought, *making Darcy feel even more embarrassed about having the kind of grandfather who surprised you after school one day with a new BMW.* It was really too wild. She tried to imagine the way she'd feel if something like that happened to her. *Talk about how the other half lives!*

"Don't suppose the old man's looking to adopt another grandkid," Caro joked, reveling in the feel of the wind twisting through her long hair.

"He's about got his hands full. My sister Sarah's twenty — that means the car she got when *she* was sixteen is about ready for a trade-in," Darcy joked back as they hit downtown Redmond.

They coasted to a stop at a red light. Caroline looked out the window at a couple of greasy-looking guys hanging out on the corner, sheltering cigarettes from the wind with cupped hands, then glanced at Darcy's poised and perfect profile. *It's too tempting — got to shake her up a little.*

"Hey there," Caro called, seeing Darcy sit bolt upright out of the corner of her eye. Caro twisted, crossing her arms along the open window and smiling in a way that she knew from experience to be irresistible. Not that these guys deserved the smile; it was just part of the game. "We've got a back seat. Looking for a ride?"

Just then the light at the intersection turned green. Darcy floored it, bouncing Caro back into her seat. "Darce, you blew it," she chided, laughing helplessly. "Two very sexy dudes and they could've been ours!"

Darcy laughed, too, though nervously. "Sexy, sure, if you like them unwashed," she said with a grimace.

Caroline grinned at Darcy's objection. "Sometimes I do," she declared breezily.

Downtown sped past in a collage of storefronts and pedestrians and windowboxes bright with geraniums and mums. On a day like this even Redmond didn't look so rotten, Caro observed. Of course, it wasn't the same riding in the passenger seat as being behind the wheel. But either way she was on the road. *Bliss*.

"So where do we go?"

"Hmm?"

"I'm not used to having my own car. Cruising," Darcy explained somewhat shyly. "Where should we drive to?"

"Where should we drive to," repeated Caro, her lips twitching in a self-conscious smile. "Me, for one, when I cruise, I don't drive *to* anywhere. I just drive."

Darcy nodded solemnly, as if she were taking mental notes: The Art of Cruising, taught by an expert.

But I end up places all the same, Caroline thought to herself. She pictured the sun rising peach and pink through the mist above the river at her favorite private spot, the turn-off over the falls. T.J. knew about it. Should she share it with Darcy? Maybe some other time . . .

Tapping her fingers on the wheel to the radio's beat, Darcy darted a mischievous look at Caro. "I wasn't going anywhere in particular. So I've been cruising without even knowing it?"

"Oh, yeah. You're a natural."

"I think I'm going to like this." Turning onto Route 11 east away from the sun, Darcy pushed her Vuarnets up on her breeze-tousled hair. "My house — sometimes I can't wait to get out of it," she confided tentatively.

"Tell me about it," said Caro with feeling. Sometimes — make that *all* the time in her case. Her father's bachelor apartment didn't feel like a home — she and her dad didn't even feel like a family since her mother ran out on them when Caroline was in fifth grade. It was mostly at night she had the urge to run away, when her father got back from the law office and Suzi, his latest bimbo girlfriend, showed up in her candy-pink Fiat. Baby talk and drunkenness — it turned her stomach. Curious, Caro studied Darcy's calm profile. Darcy couldn't have any reasons like *that* for wanting to escape the Jenner mansion. "What's your house like?" she asked.

The question was direct and personal, but Darcy didn't seem put off. "You mean, why do I want to get away from it? It'll probably sound weird. Really, I'm not even sure myself. I think it's 'cause the house is so . . . so *spotless*." Caro laughed and Darcy tried to explain. "Seriously, it's like a museum! *Formal*. I mean, my own *bedroom*. It's no fun messing it up when the maid cleans it again the minute my back's turned!"

Caro wrinkled her nose, slipping off her shoes so she could cross her feet on the seat. Imagine a *maid*! It'd be like living in a hotel. It didn't sound all that bad — still, she saw Darcy's point.

"And like, today." Darcy bit her lip, grimacing. "My parents' little afternoon sherry hour. There's no way I want to hang around in the parlor talking about absolutely nothing with them. If it wasn't for my grandfather, I wouldn't've stuck around a minute."

"What were your parents doing home, anyway?" Caro asked and then wished she hadn't when Darcy blushed again. *Nosy*. Caroline hated people who were and here *she* was, practically asking to read Darcy's diary. "Sorry," Caro added. "Don't mind me. Don't *answer* me!"

"It's okay. A fair question." Darcy laughed uncomfortably. "My parents don't exactly . . . have jobs." She put the back of one hand dramatically to her forehead. "There, our secret's out."

"They don't work at all?" *Now that's really rich*, Caroline thought, amazed.

"Well, my dad's on the board of directors of a bunch of stuff — Rhiner's Mill and all. He spends a couple hours a day with his secretary going over business. Makes a lot of phone calls. But no, he doesn't *work*. And my mother . . . " The pale blue eyes Darcy turned to Caro were amused, cynical. "She doesn't work either. She just *is*."

"And that's enough if you're a Jenner, hmm?" teased Caro.

Darcy's tone cooled slightly. "You bet."

Change the subject, Caroline ordered herself. *It's not fair putting Darce on the defensive about the family she can't help belonging to.*

Another mile slid by under the tires of the BMW, and suddenly a canopy of pumpkin-orange maple leaves overhead turned the world fourteen-karat gold. They were racing the river now, and Caro flipped off the radio so they could hear the water's chatter.

Darcy's expression had defrosted again and the momentary silence between them was peaceful and companionable. Caroline reconsidered. Maybe it *was* the right time to share her place by the falls with Darcy. "Right up here — see just past that red mailbox? Pull in the driveway and then hook left on the dirt path," Caro instructed.

Darcy did as she was told. Caro had a feeling she *always* did as she was told. Rounding a clump of birch trees, Darcy nosed the BMW up to the railing over the falls, gasping with delight at the view. "Caro, this is beautiful! I've been down this road about a zillion times — I can't believe I didn't even know this was here."

"I found it by accident," Caroline admitted. "A year or so ago when I first got the Mustang. Hey, let's get out; we can get closer to the water."

The gravel crunched under their feet as together they crossed to the rusty guard rail. They stepped over it, then slid cautiously down the grassy slope to a rock outcropping protruding right over the falls. Sheltered from the autumn breeze and warmed by the sun, the rock was just big enough for two people.

"Heaven," Darcy sighed, leaning back on her hands with her legs stretched out.

"Hmm," agreed Caro. She lay flat on her back and tipped her face sunward, half closing her eyes. "I've been thinking it'd be fun to camp out here, fall asleep to the sound of the water crashing all over the place."

"As long as you didn't toss and turn too much and roll yourself right over the cliff into the river!"

Caro laughed. "That's probably why I've only *thought* about it and never *done* it."

They were both quiet for a few minutes. The rich autumn smell of earth and fallen leaves tickled

Caroline's nostrils. An intoxicating smell, but for some reason it made her more sad than anything else. *What is it about this time of year?* She wasn't an old person, depressed by the seasons passing and all that. And she wasn't an eleven-year-old girl anymore, smashing the smiling jack-o-lantern her mother'd helped her carve just the day before and crying like she'd never stop. Aware of only one thing, that her mom was gone and wouldn't be coming back . . .

Caro sat up and grabbed a handful of dead leaves, scraping one knuckle painfully on the rough granite of the rock.

Tossed, the leaves were caught by the breeze and spun in lazy spirals until they were swallowed by the churning water. "Do you remember fifth grade?" Caroline asked casually.

She liked the way Darcy didn't act surprised, caught whatever ball you threw her. "Let's see . . . fifth grade. Green Valley Country Day School. God, Mrs. *Bosomworth.* I haven't thought about her in ages! Can you believe that was actually somebody's *name?* And of course she was — " Darcy's fingers sketched a mighty Valkyrie-type in the air. Caro hooted. "As you might imagine, none of us could say her name without cracking up, and we said it every chance we got."

"Mrs. Bosomworth!" Caro was limp from laughing.

"Mrs. Bosomworth. Sue Rhiner and I sat next to each other, and she'd make me laugh so hard, doodling well-endowed Mrs. Bosomworths in her notebook. She drew the best Mrs. Bosomworths, even better than Mike Moriarty, the prepubescent pervert."

Laughing erased the dark memories. Relaxed again, Caro lay back on the rock with her arms folded underneath her head. "I didn't think kids at the Country Day School did things like that."

"Oh, we were juvenile, too," Darcy assured her. "Probably more so 'cause the teachers were stricter. The same at boarding school. I mean, you've seen the basic prep-school equipment — trick chewing gum and super-glue! Talk about *juvenile* . . . "

"Boarding school," mused Caro. "I kind of like the idea. Gets you away from your parents."

"Not as much fun as it might seem." Darcy's mouth tightened. "All girls, remember? From seventh grade on, we didn't see a male under the age of forty until the weekly Friday night mixer with Kingsford."

"That's right. No guys — I can't even *imagine*."

"It was too strange." Darcy leaned forward to gently brush a ladybug off her knee. "I was glad to get out."

Caroline had been wondering something ever since the day Darcy waltzed into Norwell High for the first time. "How did you get yourself out, exactly?"

Shooting Caro a mischievous glance, Darcy smiled. "You'll like this story," she guessed. "I got caught with a guy in my room after visiting hours. *Way* after visiting hours! I was already on probation for leaving campus without permission a couple of times. That was the final straw."

"Darcy Jenner!" Grinning, Caro wagged a finger. "I'm shocked! I didn't think you were that kind of girl."

"I'm not," confessed Darcy. "The guy — he was from Kingsford — he was nobody special. I just did it to be rebellious. I *wanted* to get caught and kicked out. I was sick of Merton Hall."

Caro was impressed by Darcy's recklessness. It was a feeling she could relate to, no problem. "So you got caught, shall we say, *in the act*?"

"Oh, no!" The giveaway blush struck again. "The dorm proctor pounded down the door before we got much past first base." Darcy hesitated before adding, "I was glad, actually. Wasn't ready, didn't want to go through with it. Um, sex, I mean."

Seeing Darcy was embarrassed, Caroline didn't press her. She laughed the story off, saying, "Picture *me* at Merton. I'd've been kicked out after a week!"

"I lasted two whole years."

"And now you're stuck at Norwell." Caro spoke the name distastefully.

"It's like paradise after Merton, though," Darcy said. "I mean, I hated it the first couple of days, I'll admit. The Rat Pack made me miserable. But I wanted to go there. I got home from Merton ready to vaporize my parents by announcing I planned to attend public high school. Then they beat me to the punchline — they'd already signed me up!"

"Punishment for getting kicked out and all?"

Darcy lowered her eyes. "Something like that," she said in a small voice.

The sun had dipped behind the trees, leaving the rock in cold shadow. Crossing her arms, Darcy sat up. Caro nodded and got to her feet. "Let's bail."

"I should probably be heading back," Darcy said as

they climbed into the car. She revved the engine. "My parents are worse than the proctors at Merton, always wanting to know exactly where I'm going, who I'll be with, and when I'll be home."

I wonder what Darcy has told her parents about me and T.J. and Josh and Split River Station? Caro thought. *Can't imagine we'd be considered suitable. I'm no Sue Rhiner!*

Caroline allowed herself another second's thought about her own home, and realized that she probably *shouldn't* be heading back. By now her father and Suzi and maybe some of their repulsive friends were at the apartment and into their third martinis. A scene Caro definitely preferred to avoid. "Drop me off at T.J.'s, Darce?"

"Sure." Darcy hummed a few bars of the Prince tune on the radio. Then she smiled, the expression in her eyes obscured behind the dark lenses of her Vuarnets. "That's another thing. About Norwell High, I mean. *Guys.* I'm not used to being around them all the time, in class and everything. In boarding school you could never just hang out with a guy, as friends, like you and T.J."

The hint of a question lurked in Darcy's last remark. *"Friends, like you and T.J. . . . "*

For a split second, all of Caroline's defenses went up, and she felt a flicker of anger at Darcy's well-disguised prying. The old Caroline Buchanan would've kept her mouth firmly shut. She didn't have friends to confide in — she just had guys and sex. But since T.J., since she'd realized how good it could feel to open up a little, Caro had changed. Besides, she'd been asking some pretty personal questions herself about Darcy's family and such.

"Me and T.J. . . . yeah, we are just friends." Caro took a deep breath. Then, cautiously, she gave Darcy a bare-bones version of what had happened the night of the Kick-off dance, their discovery that they shared a much deeper attraction. "So, we're just friends, but there's this tension, like a bomb waiting to go off, you know?" she concluded. "Half of me is grateful. No guy's ever wanted me for *me*. The other half thinks it's a waste not to go with our feelings. The other half's . . . afraid. Of what would happen if we did . . . act. Wait — that's three halves!" Caro grinned. "No wonder I'm so confused."

They laughed together, Darcy's unspoken sympathy warmer than the sinking corn-yellow sun. *I can trust her,* Caroline thought. It was something new for her, trust, and she was still a little stiff about it. But she was willing to give it a shot.

"Caro said go for it. Act on my feelings," Darcy pep-talked herself, alone in the car fifteen minutes later. "Okay. I'm acting!"

She braked cautiously at the intersection of Coville and Seventh Street. Tacky neon lights, a scarred tarmac parking lot half full of cars and kids — Jake's Place, the burger stand where Josh worked.

Before leaving Caroline at T.J.'s, Darcy had confessed she was halfway to having a crush on Josh. Maybe crush wasn't even the right word — she just wanted to get to know him better.

"I really think you need to fortify yourself with a chocolate malt on your way home," Caro had suggested meaningfully. "And Josh mixes 'em up especially well. You order your malt, *then* you ask him what he's doing after he gets off work."

Fine advice. First, though, Darcy had to get out of the car. And walk across the parking lot.

Rolling into an empty parking space, Darcy bit her lip. Talk about standing out like your basic sore thumb. Needless to say, hers was the only BMW in the lot. Other Redmond kids drove Buicks and Fords and pickups, and they weren't brand-spanking-new, either.

This is the real world, kid, Darcy told herself as she climbed out of the car. *You asked for it — you got it.*

The real world. For most of her life, Darcy hadn't even known there was such a thing. She thought *her* world, the world of Jenners and Rhiners and their blueblood friends was the real one. Her doting overprotective parents did everything in their power to shield her from evidence to the contrary. But since Darcy had started at Norwell High, her world had changed, grown, in strange and unexpected ways. She'd stepped across some kind of line. Her parents couldn't hold their hands over her eyes anymore.

"Hey, babe, lookin' to hire a chauffeur, drive you 'round town in that pretty little car?"

To the left, through wisps of her wind-scattered hair, Darcy saw four guys lounging against the side of a cut-down yellow Chevy. What was left of the cool crowd since Shet and Leon left town — Matt, Taylor, Walt, and Art.

It was Matt who'd spoken and when Darcy didn't respond, he raised his raspy voice. "What's the deal, babe? You don't talk t' guys who ain't rich? I'm rich, I swear. Take a look at all this dough!"

Matt waved his wallet. There were guffaws and catcalls from the other guys. Her chin set, Darcy ignored them, consciously keeping her pace regular so they wouldn't have the satisfaction of knowing they spooked her.

Just past six was still early, and Darcy was the only one inside Jake's. Good, there wouldn't be any witnesses to her inexperienced flirting.

Across the buffed-steel take-out counter a pair of brown eyes met Darcy's. A short heavy-set girl tapped a stubby pencil in a bored fashion. "Can I take your order, please?"

"Oh." Darcy's smile faded. She peered discreetly over the girl's shoulder. "Um, yeah. I'd like a chocolate malt."

The girl threw together the malt ingredients, then started the shaker. At the far end of the smoky kitchen, scraping idly at the greasy grill with a spatula, was Josh. *I can't just holler at him*, Darcy decided. Dignity forbade such a display. Order something from the grill, maybe?

"Here's your malt. That's a dollar twenty."

"Oh. Uh, I also want . . . an order of fries. A small order."

The girl narrowed her eyes, why didn't you say so in the first place fashion. At a word from her, Josh dunked a basket of stringy, white, cold-looking potatoes in the deep fryer. Just as Darcy had gambled, when the fries were done Josh delivered them to the girl behind the counter, catching sight of Darcy at the same time.

"Darce, what're you doin' here?" he exclaimed, the tired, preoccupied expression melting into a shy, surprised smile.

"Dollar ninety." The girl poked a hand out for the money. Darcy paid quickly, just to get rid of her.

"Hi, Josh! Oh, I was just in the neighborhood," Darcy began. *Weak. What a line.* "I went for a drive with Caro and on my way home realized I was starving," she added. Somewhat better, but still weak.

Leaning his elbows on the counter, Josh nudged the paper bag. "Should've ordered from me. I'd've given you a large fries, no extra charge."

Darcy laughed. "I'll remember that next time."

"Yeah, do that. And hey, next time come when it's not so crowded so I can give you more personal attention," he joked.

Smiling on the outside, Darcy wondered on the inside if that was her cue to leave. Sure, Josh was kidding around with her, but there was another side to his manner. When he first saw her, behind the pleased surprise she'd sensed embarrassment, as if maybe he resented being caught in the act of working for a living.

Time to pop the question. "Um, gotta work late tonight, Josh?" Darcy asked, the paper sack in her hand.

"Till eleven." He straightened, wiping his hands on his apron. "It's not so bad," he added defensively.

"Oh." Darcy blushed. He'd taken her question all wrong. "Well, see you at school."

"Catch ya later."

She marched toward the door with her malt and fries, feeling like a remote-controlled robot. Just when she'd spent a great afternoon with Caroline and had started to feel like maybe she could fit in with this real-world business, it was like driving the BMW into a wall. A wall named Josh Hickham.

T.J. and Caro were easy, but with Josh, Darcy always felt a small but distinct tension. Josh, defensive in his grease-spattered apron and paper hat, reminded Darcy she *wasn't* one of them. She *hadn't* stepped completely over any imaginary line. She was straddling it maybe, with a foot on either side.

FOUR

T.J. crested the hill a block from Josh's house, pumping hard. Heading downhill, gravity took over the work. The bike wobbled as T.J. put his feet up on the handlebars and stuck his arms out to the side. His longish blond hair whipped in the wind. "Look at me, man!" he yodeled. "I'm flying!"

Josh watched from the end of his driveway, poised for two-wheeled flight himself. "McAllister, you *ass!*"

But T.J. miraculously made it to the Hickhams' mailbox without wiping out and splattering his brains all over Briar Street. "Piece a cake," he said cheerfully, resuming a more conventional position.

"You planning on auditioning for the circus or something?" asked Josh. Pedaling in sync, they left the horrible Hickham household behind them.

"Maybe." T.J. considered the idea with the utmost seriousness. "Why haven't I thought of a clown for a profession? A highly underrated art, if you want my opinion."

"You'd be a natural, if you want *my* opinion," Josh told him.

"Go ahead, laugh." Jumping the curb, T.J. cut the corner onto Main. "Wait'll I'm the toast of Ringling Brothers, Barnum and Bailey. Then you'll be singing a different tune!"

T.J. sliced past an elderly man on the sidewalk who was struggling to put up an umbrella. Two whole drops of rain must've fallen — obviously the old guy wasn't a native. A true Pennsylvanian, T.J. decided, would classify this as pleasant weather. He'd only lived in Redmond a couple weeks, but already T.J. had figured out that it rained at least every other day. When it didn't rain, it was usually grey. Today, though, T.J. viewed the fat, muddy clouds with tolerance, even affection. He and Josh had a place to go to get out of the rain — Split River Station.

"Whoa, here's my stop." T.J. braked in front of Pulaski's Drugstore and went in. A minute later he returned, triumphant. He flapped the latest *Superman* comic in Josh's face. "Some serious reading material. Can't fritter all my time away on Shakespeare."

As the rain was holding off, they pedaled on at a leisurely pace. T.J. was about to suggest hanging a left when he noticed Josh practically twisting his head off to stare longingly at some store window. He followed Josh's eyes: Falkowitz's Art Supplies.

T.J., riding in front of Josh, slammed on his

brakes so abruptly Josh just about rear-ended him. "Almost forgot," T.J. announced, as if just struck by a thought. "Gotta have some new number twos before I attempt my calc homework. Want to go in here?"

Did Josh ever. His eyes were like streetlights flicking on at dusk.

Then T.J. noticed the sign in the window: "Temporary Part-time Help Wanted." No way! It was like they were meant by fate to ride by Falkowitz's today. It was *ordained*.

Josh was a funny guy — it'd taken T.J. a while to decipher him. First Josh was toughing it up with the cool guys at Norwell, helping to unwelcome T.J. to Redmond in a very novel way. Then another Josh slowly emerged — shy, honest, alone. The main key to Josh's character ended up being something T.J. had never expected — Josh was a secret artist.

And here was a made-to-order opportunity to force Josh into the open, into giving his talent some air and space to grow. "Check this out, man." T.J. thumped the glass with his forefinger.

"Help wanted," Josh read out loud, his eyes glassy.

"McAllister's Instant Job Service: another satisfied customer." T.J. slapped Josh on the back. "Good-bye, burger joint!"

He saw hope on Josh's face, fighting with doubt and insecurity. *Gotta tip the scales,* he realized. "Temporary part-time help wanted — that's you, man. You got no excuse not to check it out." When Josh remained paralyzed, T.J. grabbed his jacket sleeve and yanked. "At least help me pick out my pencils, why don't you."

Inside the store was dim and cluttered and, to T.J.'s nose, malodorous. But Josh took a deep, appreciative sniff. "Fresh paper," he explained gruffly to T.J.

"Fine." T.J. kept propeling Josh forward. They passed a display of felt-tips. A pad of paper lay out on the shelf for sample pen doodles, and T.J. recognized the distinctive cartoons that could only have been drawn by Josh — boldly sketched boxes inhabited by figures, some grotesque and monstrous, others warmly human and humorous. Yep, Josh had been in there recently — T.J. knew he made the pilgrimage a couple of times a week. Josh himself looked in the direction of the sample pens and paper almost guiltily, as if he felt like some private inside part of himself had been laid bare.

They reached the counter. The scarecrow-skinny guy tending register eyed them suspiciously. "Go ahead, ask," T.J. urged Josh in a low mafioso-style voice.

"Uh . . . " Josh turned into a champion stutterer. "Th-the old man who usually w-works here . . . "

"He had a stroke. Why?"

Josh licked his cracked lips. "The j-job."

T.J. took over. "We'd like to apply," he said smoothly. "*He'd* like to apply."

"Could only be for a few months," the guy behind the counter warned. "Till the old man's ready to come back."

"Okay, by us. Right, Hickham?"

But Josh had vaporized. T.J. twisted in time to see his friend hit the sidewalk and swing a leg over his bike.

Down Main Street, a block on Seventh, a fast right onto Oak, Josh's mind pedaled as fast as his feet.

Part-time at Falkowitz's . . . hours and hours with all that paper and all those pens . . . too good to be true. Could he do it? All he had to do was fill out an application. . . . But what would people think? A job at an art supplies store — definitely soft and uncool. Jake's Place was maybe not radically interesting but somehow it was acceptable. He could hide behind the take-out counter, become anonymous. Nobody noticed the guy who handed over the fries and malts.

Josh remembered he hadn't felt anonymous the other day, though, when Darcy showed up at Jake's. He'd felt *naked*. He was wearing his greasy old apron, sure, but he was still exposed.

Josh couldn't even imagine talking to someone like Darcy about this whole job thing. How could she ever relate to his doubts and worries? Like, could he make enough money at Falkowitz's to pay the rent, and how would he survive without the free food he got at Jake's? *Imagine what it'd be like never to have to work*, he thought. *Having everything you wanted just handed to you before you even asked.*

Weeds rattled against the spokes as Josh navigated his bike across the junk-strewn empty lot next to Mr. Lee's Chinese take-out. He pictured the new BMW, gleaming in the school parking lot. No doubt about it, Darcy had it so easy it wasn't even funny.

Someone or something was crashing through the weeds behind him. Glancing over his shoulder, Josh saw T.J. charting a slalom course through the garbage cans, dodging an abandoned refrigerator with its doors gaping open. Josh slowed.

T.J. pulled up alongside him. "You heading for the station?" he shouted against the wind.

Josh nodded. "No place else to go!" It hadn't started raining for real, but Josh knew it was just a matter of time. Big fat drops the size of gum balls splashed his face every few seconds. The soggy clouds were so low they practically scraped the roofs of the tin-patched, peeling-paint houses on Cross County Road, down which they were now racing.

Josh waited for T.J. to rib him for chickening out at Falkowitz's, or to try pumping up his self-confidence with an inspirational speech.

Instead T.J. yelled, "Women," like the concept was occurring to him for the first time.

"Huh?"

"There'll be a couple," T.J. elaborated at the top of his voice. "At the station."

Josh was interested. "Yeah? Who?" he shouted casually.

"Caro and Darcy are initiating Alison to the joys of trespassing." Wheel to wheel, T.J. and Josh skidded off Cross County Road and cut across the fields toward Split River Station, going direct, as the crow flies. "Couldn't have 'em outnumbering us so I told Marc Calamano to stop by after practice. He and I gotta work on our Shakespeare project anyhow. It's scheduled for tomorrow."

Marc, the football jock. Josh knew him slightly. A nice guy, as big as a building. But forget Marc — Alison Laurel! Gritting his teeth against the raw wind, Josh concentrated on keeping his face from splitting into an ear-to-ear grin.

"There's something about Alison . . ." Josh began. The wind snatched the words from his mouth and whirled them around like a handful of dry leaves. Josh couldn't believe he'd made such a confession.

But T.J. was cool. "You're right. There *is* something about Alison," he agreed, kicking his bike across the disused railroad tracks that spun a web around Split River Station.

The hunter-green BMW was pulled up on the east side of the station, its gloss a sharp contrast to the crumbling brick. For an instant, Josh felt a flash of resentment. With that car and an entire mansion to mess around in, Darcy Jenner didn't *need* Split River Station. What was she doing here anyway?

He shook the unreasonable thought out of his head as T.J. opened the station door. "Hey, is this where Girl Scout troop twelve is meeting?" T.J. inquired.

Josh heard Caroline's rich laugh. "If Girl Scouts was like *this*, I might have joined!"

The instant Josh stepped into the station, he saw and heard and smelled *Alison*. The music pulsing from the boombox was Alison; the spicy-woodsy incense was Alison. Alison herself was curled on the sofa, her slim legs tucked up under a bulky purple sweater.

Caroline and Darcy lounged on either side of the ember-warm space heater. "What's up?" T.J. asked, fielding the bag of chips Caro tossed his way and then passing it to Josh.

"Trading recipes," Darcy joked, her smile welcoming and warm and spontaneous. Josh smiled back, munching guilt along with a fistful of potato chips. *Darcy belongs as much as I do*, he acknowledged to himself silently.

Caroline smiled as T.J. squished himself next to her in the rickety lounge chair. Josh stalled. The obvious place for *him* to sit was . . . with Alison. He rocked back on his heels, gathering emotional momentum. Then he took a deep breath and dove. Surfaced on the couch.

Now what? Josh said the first dumb thing that came to mind. "Chips?" he offered, holding out the bag.

Alison took one chip, delicately. "Thanks."

Josh willed someone else to talk so he wouldn't have to.

Caroline started the ball rolling. "So now that you've been here ten minutes, what do you think, Mouse?"

Alison's brown velvet eyes were wide as she gazed around the station. "I love it. It's cold" — she had her arms wrapped tightly around her drawn-up knees — "but it's *warm*. I can see a little bit of all of you here."

And now a little bit of you . . . Josh felt himself relax, his spine collapsing, melted by Alison's gentle voice.

His reverie was interrupted as he realized someone was pounding on the door.

"Who's there?" T.J. called.

"Me, Marc," answered a deep voice on the other side of the door.

"Get in here, Calamano!"

Josh didn't think the door was going to be big enough, but by stooping slightly Marc made it through. He shrugged, his shoulders about half a mile wide under his Norwell High varsity jacket. His hair was wet, from the rain or a post-practice shower. "Guess I got the address right," he joked, his voice amiable and slow.

"How did you get here?" asked T.J.

"Dad was using the truck so I hitched." A grin creased Marc's handsome face. "Caught a semi headin' north up fifty-eight. Driver thought I was some kinda psycho-killer, asking to get out in the middle of nowhere."

T.J. played the role of host. "You know everyone?"

"Um . . . sort of." The grin again, disarming. "Hi, Caroline. Hickham. And Darcy, right?" Marc's eyes settled on Alison. "And you're . . . "

"Alison. Hi," she said, her tone friendly.

"That's right," Caroline observed. "Theater arts and sports don't usually mix."

"Yeah, we've got a genuine melting pot here," T.J. agreed. "You bring ol' *Macbeth*?"

While T.J. and Marc started rapping about their Shakespeare presentation, Alison turned to Josh. "How's the world treating you?" she asked, as if she really wanted to know.

"All right." Looking into Alison's eyes, Josh realized he didn't have to hand her a line. Didn't have to say things were okay if they weren't. "Well, could be better. But I got an idea today. About switching jobs, doing something I like with my time for a change . . ."

Josh was ready to rashly share the whole story with Alison when yet another McAllister brainstorm struck.

"I got it!" T.J. announced. "Marc could use some tips on reading his part for tomorrow. And right here we have our very own rising star of the theater arts, Alison Mouse Laurel! Man, I'm so *smart*."

Alison laughed and Marc shrugged, looking a little rueful but not uneasy. "You need a drama coach?" she asked, her voice encouraging.

"*Macbeth*, act one, scene three. You know it?"

"'If chance will have me king, why, chance may crown me,'" Alison quoted, reverent.

"Hey, that's my line," said T.J., grinning.

"Well, I'm just Angus," Marc explained. "I've only got a couple of lines. But as McAllister can tell you, I butcher the ol' Bard something fierce. I could use some help."

"You're on." Alison looked around the dim, dusky station. "Let's drag a few chairs over there, okay?"

Josh watched. Marc Calamano didn't have to *drag* any chairs. The jock gripped a lounge and the bean-bag in one hand, his Shakespeare book cradled in the other. Then he and Alison retreated to a corner of the room and put their heads together.

Josh kept watching out of the corner of his eye.

Meanwhile Darcy had lit a few candles. Was it just the flickering, suggestive light? No, there was definitely something about their body language. The way Alison looked up at Marc as she talked about rhythm and inflection. The way Marc leaned over her, attentive, protective.

They made it look so easy to be close. Josh was stabbed by a sense of inadequacy. He could hardly bring himself to *talk* to a girl he liked. Not that Marc was coming on to Alison; it might not exactly be love at first sight. An arty girl and a jock? Unlikely. But Josh would've bet a week's paycheck something had just clicked between them.

FIVE

Three strikes, I'm out, Darcy thought, watching Josh watch Marc and Alison. *Josh does indeed have a thing for Alison, that's plain.*

She shivered, edging her chair closer to the space heater. She didn't care enough to be jealous; her little crush on Josh hadn't gone far. Besides, she really liked Alison. Still, a twinge of *something* nagged at Darcy's heart.

It wasn't just that Josh went moony when he talked to Alison. It was *how* he talked to her. Eager and unrestrained. With her, on the other hand, he was friendly but cautious, his eyes wary. Every now and then those eyes opened up to Darcy, and Josh looked at her with the sort of light she'd seen him cast on Alison. But just as fast they'd shut down again.

When that happened Darcy got an uncanny feeling, like she'd been caught doing something wrong, *being* something wrong. Caught eating with her fingers at a high-society banquet, or asking for a wine list at a diner. Caught being the wrong person in the right place. Or was it the right person in the wrong place? Off base, whatever.

T.J. was practicing his own lines from *Macbeth*, soliloquizing to a poster of Jim Morrison. Stretching her arms over her head, Caroline yawned. "This literary scene is too thick for me," she said to Darcy. "Want to take off? Go cruising in your auto?"

Darcy flicked her eyes from Caro to Josh and back again. She was definitely up for leaving. "Sounds good."

Slipping into her leather bomber jacket, Darcy only half noticed the look that passed between T.J. and Caroline — questioning on his part, careless on Caro's. Josh, now stretched full length on the sofa, pseudo-napping, cracked open an eye. "So long."

Outside the rain clouds had been pushed east by a clean west wind. The BMW sparkled in the cold sun, inviting.

"Where to?" Darcy asked Caroline, skidding the car off the sand of the side road onto the black-topped highway. "Oh, that's right. Almost forgot. Cruising means not going anywhere in particular."

Caro laughed. "Well, that's the general rule. But there are exceptions. Like right now." She checked the digital clock on the dashboard. "Five-thirty. Happy hour — when they punch the clock at the mill. Everyone's heading to the strip. Let's go downtown and check out the action."

"The strip?" Darcy repeated casually, not wanting to let on she didn't know exactly what Caroline was talking about.

"Nordecke Street, west of Main. The bars," Caroline explained.

Nordecke Street — my parents would kill me! Darcy thought, exhilarated. Redmond didn't get much seedier than Nordecke west of Main. *The strip . . .*

Lit by the low sun, the buildings of the town stood out in dramatic relief against the purple wall of retreating clouds. And Caro was right. While the Main Street stores were closed up for the night, things were alive on the strip.

Caro shot down her window and Darcy did the same. Cold air tangled their hair. "Red lights," said Caro as they pulled up at one, "are the worst when you're in the mood to move. But if you want to meet guys . . ."

They were in the left lane. A souped-up black Trans Am rumbled up on the right and Darcy saw what Caro meant. Flipping her hair over one shoulder, Caro reached out the window and tapped the Trans Am's side mirror. "Nice wheels," she commented, her eyes warm and her smile cool.

The guy driving the Trans Am grinned. "Like yours, too," he said, talking around an unfiltered cigarette. "And I like your chauffeur."

Darcy giggled. She couldn't seem to get away from chauffeur jokes — and probably wouldn't until she traded the BMW for a pickup.

"Hey, chauffeur," the guy called, his grey eyes narrowed against the sun. The cigarette dangled miraculously from his lower lip. "When the boss lets you off work, wanna drive my car for a while? I see you know how to handle a stick but" — his voice became warm, teasing — "maybe you could use some advanced lessons."

The other guys in the Trans Am whistled and hooted. Darcy leaned across Caro to smile at the dude. "I can handle a stick all right," she purred. "I've got a *waiting* list of guys who want driving lessons from *me*. I'll put you on the bottom. Later, boys!" She blew him a kiss. The light changed and the BMW surged out ahead of the Trans Am.

Caro waved them off, leaning out her window, grinning. "Such talk from a Merton Hall girl," she teased.

"A *former* Merton Hall girl!" Darcy reminded her. But her heart was racing as fast and cool as the BMW's engine, revved by her own boldness. "I might be new at this," she said, "but I'm willing to learn."

"Then step on it. I think I recognize that pickup. Can you catch it?"

Darcy did, at the next light. "How'd you know he'd be so cute?" she asked Caro, checking out the guy behind the wheel.

"Brad Gradowski — he's an old friend," Caro said casually. "Hey, Brad!"

The guy turned, looking down at them. A smile of recognition creased his tanned, rugged face. "Caroline Buchanan! Where've you been hiding yourself, sweetheart?"

"I'm still just a schoolgirl, remember?" she responded, kind of flirtatiously Darcy thought. "I've got homework every single night."

"Well, skip the books tonight, babe. I'm grabbing a burger at Jake's, then headin' to McSweeney's. Why don't you and your little friend" — he gave Darcy an appraising once-over — "come on over?"

"Oh, I don't know . . . " Caroline shot Darcy a questioning look. Darcy tried not to look too panicked at the thought of going to a bar. It was one thing to drive *through* the bad part of town, playing games from your car. Another to actually walk into McSweeney's, which had a reputation for being one of the seediest places around.

Caro must have read something in Darcy's face. She shook her head at Brad. "We feel like keeping on the move," she told him. "Maybe later, okay?"

A green light, and Darcy stepped on the gas. "That okay with you?" Caro asked her.

"Sure." Darcy aimed for an airy, nonchalant tone. "But we could go to McSweeney's. If you want."

"It's nothing special," Caroline said. "We'd probably just get carded and be totally humiliated. It's just a bunch of mill guys smoking and pounding beers and watching football on the tube anyway."

Mill guys . . . "Does Brad work at Rhiner's Mill?" asked Darcy, curious.

"No. He's been helping on his dad's farm since he graduated from Norwell two years ago. He's a pretty good guy."

Looping around the block to head back up Nordecke, Darcy thought about Brad, sitting high in his pickup, a six o'clock shadow darkening his face.

Imagine graduating from high school and then going straight to work, on a farm or at the mill! Whether or not Darcy was going to college wasn't even a question. Her older sister Sarah was at Smith in Massachusetts. Their mother had gone there, and their grandmother and their great-grandmother — Smith already had a place reserved for Darcy in next year's freshman class. As for working at the mill, she didn't personally know anyone who did. Sue's father didn't exactly count, seeing as how he *owned* the place.

One by one the streetlights fizzled on. Suddenly Darcy realized it was night. Her eye darted to the clock on the dashboard and she gulped. It was dinner hour at home — her parents would be starting the meal without her, getting ready to give her the third degree when she walked through the door.

It would be a repeat of the same conversation she'd had with them every day for weeks: Where was she all day? With that Caroline Buchanan, whose father was a low-life labor lawyer and a lush, to boot? Why wasn't she hanging out with Sue Rhiner anymore? Why wasn't she spending more time on her school work? Etc., etc.

It seemed like ever since she'd moved back home from Merton, she hadn't been able to do one thing right in her parents' eyes. They jumped on her for every word out of her mouth, even if she wasn't talking back. Maybe it was because this was the first time in years the three of them had actually lived together for more than a three-week stretch. She'd been in boarding school since the seventh grade, and her summers had been spent at riding camp or tennis camp or Grandpa Jenner's beach house. Now the three of them were a family again, and as far as she could tell, her parents were finding their youngest daughter quite unsatisfactory.

Well, then I'll be unsatisfactory, she thought angrily as a feeling of pure rebellion rushed through her.

"Darce?" Caro's voice sounded uncertain. "You okay? You seemed to drift off a little, there."

"I'm fine," Darcy answered. And she was. She *liked* cruising. She wanted to be a party girl, like Caro. She needed some "experience," that was for sure. It was time to be naughty after so many boring years of being good.

Still, inside Darcy was nervous. *Face it, Jenner. You'd have had heart failure if Caro accepted Brad's invitation! You wouldn't have known what the hell to do at McSweeney's.* The only bars Darcy had ever been in were fancy hotel bars, where if you were underage you ordered fancy hotel bar drinks like a Virgin Mary or a strawberry daiquiri without the liquor.

"Caro, I hate to wimp out, but I really should get home," Darcy heard herself say, and hated herself for saying it. "I can take you home. . . . "

"Why don't you just drop me off at Jake's?" suggested Caro. "I can hitch a ride from Brad."

Darcy felt her face crinkle in a look of scandalized surprise. Caroline looked calmly back at her, her cool eyes golden and unreadable.

It's none of my business what Caro does with her time, Darcy reminded herself. *It's not like she's mar-*

*ried to T.J., and besides even if she was, it's not like
I'm her mother. Oops.* Darcy felt bad, even thinking
such a thing. Caroline didn't have a mother, and she
might as well not have a father. Maybe that was why
she never seemed to have any place to go. Nobody was
waiting for *her* to check in at home.

Suddenly, Darcy almost looked forward to arguing
with her parents. Home was structure, home was
safety. She wasn't ready to be free of it yet.

The parking lot at Jake's was half full. Pellets of rain
kept people inside cars and pickups, cigarette smoke
and heavy-metal music pressing against the closed
windows.

Caroline spotted Brad's blue Ford. "Sure you don't
want to join us for a burger?" she asked Darcy, knowing what the answer would be.

"No . . . thanks." Darcy's dark slender eyebrows
curved into question marks. "Sure *you* don't want a
ride home? Or . . . a ride to T.J.'s?"

Caro bit her lip sharply, resenting Darcy's not-so-
subtle hint, the moralistic Priscilla Alden puritan expression on her face. *You're still just a boarding-school
prude, Darcy Jenner,* she almost snapped.

Combing her tangled hair with her fingers, Caro
waited for her patience and fairness to reassert themselves. Of course Darcy couldn't understand her mo-
tives, why she did things; Caro herself didn't
understand.

"Darce." Caroline's eyes softened. "This was fun.
Driving around . . . thanks." It wasn't quite the same

as being on her own, independent and alone on the road in her Mustang. But in some ways, Caro realized with surprise, it was better. It was nice having some-one to talk to and something else to think about be-sides your own depressing thoughts.

Darcy shrugged, her hands still clenching the leath-er-encased steering wheel. "We'll do it again sometime soon."

The door to the BMW shut with a muffled, satisfy-ing thunk. Standing in the parking lot, her shoulders hunched against the rain, Caro waved once at the departing car.

Hands pushed deep in the pockets of her jeans, Caroline walked slowly across the lot toward the blue pickup. Through the fogged-up windows she could see Brad and another guy. But the face etched vividly on her brain was T.J.'s.

Why'd I give him that look? she wondered, remem-bering the wordless exchange as she left the station with Darcy. *Am I turning into a tease?*

It'd been more than teasing — she'd been taunt-ing T.J. The look had said just what she wanted it to say: "I'm going looking for a good time. Catch you later, pal." And his look had said just as clearly: "Why?"

It's your own fault, McAllister. Your own dumb fault, Caro thought defensively. T.J. had named the game — "let's be friends first" and all that — he couldn't blame her for playing it. If she and T.J. were just friends, well that meant she could still flirt with and date any guy she wanted to. She hadn't planned to bump into Brad tonight but she did, and there was nothing — nobody — standing between her and a good time.

She tapped on the driver's side window. "Hey, Gradowski. Let me in, I'm soaked!"

Brad pushed open the door. "Caroline! Climb in."

Caro bent, her wet hair swinging forward. Brad and a guy she knew slightly, Joe Anderson, were listening to a country-and-western station with a six-pack of beer between them. "There room for me?"

"You bet." Brad grabbed Caro and pulled her across his lap. "For you, we'll put the beer on the floor," he joked.

"What a tribute!" Caro winked at Joe, who handed her a cold, sweating bottle. "I see you guys still drink the finest."

"The champagne of beers," Brad agreed, his smile fast and warm.

Caroline smiled back, relaxed. It was steamy in the cab of the truck. Smelled homey, like beer and old vinyl and wet denim. And Brad was a nice guy, not like some of the jerks she'd dated. No pretensions and no hang-ups. Just an uncomplicated farm boy. He wasn't T.J., though. . . .

What am I, in love with him? Yeah, I am, Caro realized, her palm feeling suddenly hot against the icy bottle she was holding. She *was* "in love" with T.J., whatever that meant. She was in love with him and she was running away from him. Running away from love. Because love wasn't smart. The whole sex thing — that was only part of it. You could be intimate with somebody, and not let them ever really touch you inside. It'd been that way with her and Leon. But T.J. was different; he'd touched her inside before he'd ever touched her outside. And that new kind of sharing — Caro found herself craving it, needing it, and it scared her.

Much better to while away a rainy night over beers and burgers with a guy like Brad. Brad's hazel eyes were friendly, admiring. It'd been nearly a year since they'd hung out together, and he seemed really glad to see her. He'd think of a way to ditch Joe pretty soon so they could be alone. And that was okay with her.

Caro raised the bottle. "To the weather."

Brad took a pull on his beer. "Yeah, rain. Something new!"

"Seven, eight, nine . . . " T.J. counted out loud. "*Ten.*" He slammed down the receiver with a muffled curse. He wanted to shout out his frustration, but his parents were in bed. They both worked, had to get up early, and would *not* appreciate having their slumbers disturbed by an infantile tantrum.

"Go ahead, McAllister, look at the clock one more time," T.J. muttered to himself. "Make yourself suffer. It's twelve midnight and she's not home."

He knocked his head lightly against the wall next to the phone. Then he opened the fridge for about the hundredth time in the last hour, peering at the contents sightlessly. Then he reached again for the phone.

No way, man, he thought, dropping his hand. He'd

already dialed Caro's number twenty times since dinner. *There ain't gonna be no answer.*

T.J. turned his back on the phone, with an effort. If he relocated to his bedroom, maybe the temptation to keep dialing the same seven digits over and over in an obsessed psycho-killer fashion would be gone. By far the sanest move, he decided.

Upstairs, though there wasn't a phone, T.J. still had his imagination. And his memory, of Caro's eyes before she left the station that afternoon with Darcy.

Their warm greeny-gold color had hardened to I'm-going-my-own-way grey. T.J. knew that look. It was as much a part of Caroline as her laughter and the gentler, more open expressions. This look tantalized at the same time it firmly closed a door right in your face.

He kicked off his shoes and threw himself on the bed. Closing his eyes, he willed himself to be cool. "It's none of your business, anyway," he pointed out to himself. "If Caro wants to go cruising with Darcy, she's got a right. If she stays out till dawn, which by the way she has a habit of doing, she doesn't owe you any explanation."

A picture popped into T.J.'s mind. He felt like he was looking at a snapshot, it was so distinct. His first impression of Caroline. His first day at Norwell, when she walked into thin-lipped Mrs. Simison's homeroom with her then-main man Leon Fiero. Leon, one possessive hand on Caro's shoulder, and the way she looked back at him. An affectionate reminder: *You don't own me.*

Nobody owned Caroline Buchanan, T.J. had

learned. Not her boyfriend, not her hard-working, hard-playing father, most of all not the mother who'd deserted her when she was a kid. Yet in a way, her mother did own Caroline — it was because of her that Caro refused to trust, to lean on anyone for more than a millisecond.

"I'm trying to understand," T.J. whispered to an absent Caro. "I'm really trying."

Rolling over and mummifying himself in the bedspread, T.J. buried his face in the pillow. Another picture was now slicing into his brain and making him crazy. Caro, that night at the station after the Kick-off Dance. All their volcanic attraction for each other had burst to the surface and they were kissing. It was amazing, the kind of kissing that definitely was not meant to be an end in itself. T.J. had wanted to follow it through — more than he'd ever wanted anything. And, miraculously, Caro had, too. In typical up-front fashion, she'd come right out and said so.

"And I said no. God, what an idiot!" T.J. groaned into the pillow. "The most outrageously beautiful girl in the world says 'I'm yours.' And I say, no thanks, I'll take a rain check."

Now that night appeared to T.J. like a winning lottery ticket torn in two and flushed down the toilet. He'd had a chance, sex or no sex, to press Caro for a commitment, to make her his.

"And where do you think she'd be right now if you did?" he asked himself. "You jerk, she'd be right where she is now, wherever the hell that is. *Not* with you, anyhow."

He remembered Caroline at Split River Station, with the rain pounding on the roof like a heavy-metal drum solo. Willing, loving, vulnerable. Passionate but still proud. And separate. Always, no matter how close their bodies were, a kind of shield or something around her. And if he ever tried to take away that space, T.J. knew he'd chase her away for good.

SIX

"No, sir, I think *you're* the one making a mistake. Yes, I *will* be taking my business elsewhere from now on!" The Jenners' cook slammed down the phone indignantly, and Darcy, swinging her legs from a high stool at the kitchen counter, burst out laughing.

Colleen scowled. "I don't see the joke, Darcy Ellen Jenner. You're not the one that has to go through the Yellow Pages now looking for another liquor store that'll deliver in an hour!"

Darcy laughed harder, holding her sides. "What a hardship. The Yellow Pages, all that dirty newsprint on your fingers!"

"I'll wear my work gloves to turn the pages, of course," Colleen said, grinning. Then she shook her head. "Saying we didn't pay our bill. You'd've thought I wanted to charge the whole damn *store*, not just a few bottles of sherry!"

Darcy watched Colleen polish the sterling tea set, thinking. This liquor store scuffle reminded her of another recent incident. . . . That was it, Redmond Hills Country Club, the time she went there with Caroline and the dining room wouldn't serve them. They gave Darcy some line about her family's tab being a couple of months past due; it was pretty irritating. *I better remember to tell Dad about this,* Darcy decided, making a mental note. *His secretary's screwing up somewhere, paying bills late or something.*

Just then the phone rang. Darcy looked at Colleen, who looked back at her. Colleen held up hands encased in yellow latex gloves and dripping with silver polish suds. *Probably for me anyway,* Darcy thought. Leaning forward, she reached for the receiver.

"Hello?"

"Darce? It's Caro."

"Hi. What's going on?"

"Nothing yet but I was thinking maybe tennis at the high-school courts. You up for a game?"

It was tempting. The afternoon was sunny and Indian-summer warm, and Caroline was fun to rally with. Plus, maybe Caro was ready to talk about this new Brad Gradowski development. At school that day, she'd brushed off Darcy's questions with, "Oh, nothing much happened."

"I'd really like to," Darcy told Caro regretfully. "But I sort of have to be at this thing at my house this afternoon. At four my mother's hostessing a" — she groaned — "D.A.R. tea and, well — "

"D.A.R.?"

"Daughters of the American Revolution," Darcy explained, embarrassed just to pronounce the pompous title of the organization.

Caroline's laughter crinkled warmly across the line. "I know what it *means*, Darce. I just never actually *knew* anybody who belonged!"

"Well, today's your lucky day — now you do. My mom's president of the local chapter. Me and my sister are both members. Silly, huh?"

"What's the point of it?" asked Caro in typically blunt fashion. "You just sit around and compare family trees?"

"It's a lot of stupid and boring stuff," Darcy conceded. "But they also do some real things — supporting historical-type associations and giving out educational scholarships and the like."

"Yeah, I know about that," Caroline said. "Every year they give some senior at Norwell a prize for having straight A's and being a good citizen and stuff like that. The D.A.R. Award — Margery Albright's a shoo-in this year."

"She's practically campaigning for it," Darcy agreed. "But I've gotta run. Catch you at school, okay?"

"Bye, Darce."

Replacing the receiver, Darcy took an amaretto biscuit from the pyramid carefully arranged on a silver tray. Munching it, she turned on her heel and strolled toward the door, careful not to scatter any crumbs on Colleen's spotless floor.

"I hope you're going to change your clothes," Colleen called after her.

She'd been planning to; ripped jeans and a cropped sweater that showed her navel weren't exactly appropriate for a D.A.R. tea. "Yes, I'm going to change," Darcy assured Colleen, her eyes teasing. "Into the new black leather minidress Caro helped me pick out at the mall. And no bra, of course."

From the hall Darcy heard Colleen's huff of outraged propriety, but she knew Colleen was smiling. Darcy huffed back and then pounded up the back staircase, three steps at a time.

Her bedroom, the only lived-in room on the long hallway of the east wing second floor, was neat and dust-free as usual, thanks to the maid. Suddenly, the silent impersonal tidiness seemed too oppressive for words. Darcy hit the power on her stereo receiver and shoved the volume way up. She jumbled the row of stuffed animals on the bookshelf — they looked like they were in the *military*. Stripping off her clothes, she tossed them at random. Then, in her underwear, she faced her cavernous closet.

Shirts and sweaters in a row on top, arranged by color. Skirts below. Everyday dresses in the middle, plastic-bagged formal dresses on the right. Darcy hadn't even known where to *hang* the leather dress — it didn't fall into any of her old wardrobe categories.

A wicked smile tickled the corners of her mouth. What if she did show up at the tea wearing black leather? With her hair teased out like a rock star and gobs of makeup in various shades of neon? Darcy pictured the prim and proper old Daughters of the American Revolution fainting into their Earl Grey.

And her mother, purple in the face with suppressed fury.

Sighing, Darcy pulled a slim grey wool skirt from its hanger. She added a forest-green cashmere sweater and her short strand of pearls. Stockings and pumps.

The Uniform, Darcy thought, staring with disgust into the mirror at her own reflection. The kind of outfit she'd worn every single day at Merton Hall. The kind of outfit Daughters of the American Revolution wore for life. The kind of outfit that had made her feel like a misfit when she started school at Norwell High.

"You aren't missing too much," Sue Rhiner told Darcy. "Although senior year's a gas. Liberty and license, you know? It went to Maggie Overlander's head. She made a pass at Mr. Swanson. Art history, remember? Supposedly he responded in kind — he's been given notice, anyway. And Maggie's kicked out. She always was a slut. Oh, and Alicia Kincaid got a transfer student for a roommate! This awful Irish Catholic type from some convent or other. Alicia's making the poor girl miserable. Trick gum, superglue — the works!"

Why aren't I finding this hilarious? Darcy wondered, watching her best friend struggle to swallow her giggles. Darcy managed a smile; lots of teeth but no feeling. Then an image of John Travolta in a sappy seventies-style movie popped into her head. *That's it — I feel like the boy in the plastic bubble. I'm in here*

*and they're out there. I can see them but I can't really
touch them.*

She looked around her, suddenly seeing with different eyes. The scene was so familiar and yet so strange;
it almost looked like a movie set, where objects and
actors just pretended to be real. The spacious sunny
parlor was spotless from the Persian carpet to the brass
wall sconces and dust-free family portraits. Two dozen
women and girls, including Sue, who drove down
from Merton for this thing, perched stiffly on velvet-
upholstered chairs, sipping daintily at tea and sherry
and nibbling tiny sandwiches and scones. Everyone,
old and young, wore some variation of the Uniform.

Darcy spread preserves on a scone, trying to ana-
lyze her feelings. There was something unbearably
constricting about the atmosphere and the whole situation, every aspect of it. But at the same time, it was
seductive — it was comfortable. It was what she'd
always known. *Do I love it? Hate it? Am I really so
different?*

From across the room, she caught her mother's
eye. Mrs. Jenner smiled, her expression warm and
fond. Obviously she was pleased to see Darcy with
Sue, the kind of acquaintance she thoroughly ap-
proved of.

"But what about you?" Sue went on. "You're the
one with stories to tell. We haven't gossiped in the
longest time — that's why I moved these chairs out of
earshot of all the old biddies. Tell me *all* about public
school!"

Darcy turned her eyes on Sue. Sue hadn't
changed, but then why should she? Sue would never

change, she'd just age, slowly and gracefully. Sue was perfect — the cream of the crop, the apple of everybody's eye. Her frosted blond hair, neatly pulled back by a velvet headband, didn't have one split end. Her skin was perpetually tanned golden, courtesy of the beach in the summer and various ski and Club Med weekends in the winter. Very little makeup — just a touch of mascara and shell-pink lip gloss. The Uniform. Sue was like an advertisement for the Good Life. Merton Hall put pictures of girls like Sue in its catalogue in order to lure more girls like Sue to attend.

"Public school, huh? You really want the gory details?" teased Darcy.

Sue nodded, her lips pursed in a commiserating grimace. "Is it a nightmare? I've been feeling for you, Darcy. When you told me about those revolting girls . . . "

The last time Darcy had really talked with Sue was at the start of the school year when Holly Vickers and the Rats were terrorizing her. "Oh, things have calmed down," said Darcy. "I actually kind of like it now. I figured it'd just be a matter of time, and I was right. I've met some pretty great people."

Sue looked dubious. "Ha-ha, Darcy. No, but seriously."

"I *am* serious. I like Norwell."

Sue shook her head. "I don't believe you. How can you like it? It's so . . . I don't know, so bourgeois."

"You'd be surprised," Darcy said sarcastically. "The kids there don't have B.O. and most of them can speak in complete sentences."

"You know what I *mean*."

"Yeah, I *do* know what you mean." *Only too well.* Darcy stirred some sugar into her tea, feeling sort of sick. Sure, she knew what Sue meant, because she'd inherited the same snobbery and the same prejudices. She was still struggling to leave that mindset behind.

Unwrapping an amaretto biscuit, Sue eyed Darcy. "Okay, I'll be open-minded," she said, her tone conciliatory. "You like Norwell. You've made some friends. Like who? Anyone I know?"

"Actually . . . maybe. Caroline Buchanan? I thought she mentioned once that she dated your brother or something."

"You're *not* hanging around with *Caroline Buchanan*." A statement, not a question.

Darcy bristled. "As a matter of fact, I am. Why so shocked, Sue?"

"Oh, come on, Darcy!" Sue exclaimed. "Don't play dumb. Caroline Buchanan has a statewide reputation. Frederick's not the only guy who's cashed in on her lack of morals."

"So not everyone wears a chastity belt like you!" Darcy snapped indignantly. "Caro happens to be a friend of mine. I'm sorry she doesn't meet the Rhiner standards."

Sue lifted her hands, placating. "Hey, don't be so defensive. I'm not criticizing *you*."

"Aren't you?"

"No, Darcy, really," Sue said, sounding genuinely apologetic. "It came out wrong. But if you want my opinion, which you probably don't . . . the people you hang out with and the kind of reputations they have reflect on you. I thought I'd never say this, but — you know what Mrs. Bradstreet always says about the difference between a woman and a lady."

Darcy snorted. "I don't go to Merton anymore, remember?" *Why do I keep having to remind people of that fact? Why can't I simply cut myself off from goddamn Merton and everything it stands for?*

"It doesn't matter," Sue persisted. "We're talking about standards — not just Rhiner standards but *Jenner* standards. I know you, Darcy. I've known you forever. You're not like Caroline Buchanan. And if you really think about it, you'll realize you don't want to be."

Darcy heaved a sigh, pretending to be bored in order to end the conversation. Maybe it was time to ditch Sue and find some harmless old biddy to chat with. Sue was annoying. Even worse, Sue was *right*.

"You're not like Caroline Buchanan. . . . you don't want to be . . . " *Why didn't I have a comeback for that superbitch remark?* Darcy wondered miserably. *Why didn't I say, "I'd rather be like Caro than like you any day!"?*

Because it wasn't entirely true. Darcy wasn't going to admit it to Sue — Sue would just get righteous. But inside Darcy knew she *didn't* want to be exactly like Caroline. Caro's attitudes and the fast, hard pace of her life intimidated Darcy at the same time they appealed to her.

Right then Darcy almost wished she hadn't been introduced to the new world of Nowhere High.

The D.A.R., the tea, Sue . . . stuffy, yes. But also —
safe.

Darcy looked at her mother. Mrs. Jenner was leaning against the tall bay window, framed by filmy
sunlit curtains. A charming smile for her guests, small
talk bubbling like champagne. No one who looked at
her would ever know that an hour ago she'd been in a
total snit. It began when Darcy told her about Colleen and the liquor store — the way her mother had
exploded, it almost seemed like Darcy was to blame.
And maybe, Darcy thought, *that's the way she actually sees it. If she was on edge, it probably had nothing to do with the liquor order. It's probably because
she knew all the ladies at the tea were going to be
talking about her behind her back, saying what a
lousy job she did raising me. After all, the whole
world knows I've been kicked out of Merton, and
something like that always reflects on the sacred Jenner name.*

It was the difference between surface and sub-
stance, Darcy realized, recalling how her mother
had softened when Darcy appeared for the tea all
dolled up, and even deigned to smile at her when she
was talking to Sue. As long as the outside looked
okay, nobody knew or cared what went on underneath.

Darcy shifted in her straight-backed chair, suddenly uncomfortable. She felt like a person wearing
clothes that didn't quite fit. No, it went even deeper
than that. *It's like my skin doesn't quite fit. I'm not
me.*

Sue was chattering again, more Merton gossip and

how all the girls really missed Darcy — it wasn't the same without her. Sue . . . they'd probably always be friends; they went back such a long way together, and Sue was loyal, Darcy had to give her that much. But Sue was still Merton Hall personified, everything Darcy wanted to put behind her.

And she was doing it; she'd moved beyond Sue. Still, Darcy was painfully conscious she wasn't yet on a level with Caro, T.J., and Josh. She'd put on an act cruising with Caro the day before and she was putting on an act now.

SEVEN

"Joshua, I hope you're listening to me!" the Witch screeched. Her piercing voice travelled from the kitchen to Josh's bedroom with so much force you'd think she was using a bullhorn. "Your father will hear about it if I get home from the contest and you haven't done what I asked!"

If you ever asked instead of ordered, maybe I would listen, Josh wanted to shout back.

Lying on his rumpled bed, he pressed hands to ears. But the high-pitched voice still got through. Josh would bet money that dogs all over the neighborhood were yowling in pain.

"The patio furniture has to be stored in the crawl space. The whole downstairs needs vacuuming. Kyler gets a story and a snack at four. Do you think you can manage that, Joshua? Am I asking too much of a busy, important person like you? Do you think you could do something for somebody else just this once?"

The Witch's humor was about as subtle as a drill sergeant's. Josh didn't bother with a reply — it was a waste of breath usually. Then the door to his bedroom banged open.

Not Kyler, but the other half-brat, the tiny Woman of the Hour. Five-year-old Whitni, smothered in pink frills and lace, her Shirley Temple curls stiff with hair spray and studded with satin bows, primed for her zillionth baby beauty contest. She stood with tiny hands on tiny hips, souring her candied image by poking out her tongue.

"My momma's talking to you," Whitni lisped, a miniature Witch-in-training. "You'd better listen. Aren't you going to wish me good luck?"

Josh stared dully at Whitni. All of a sudden he got the point of that dark, bitter Stones song, "Paint it Black." If he'd had a brush and a can of paint of the appropriate color, he'd have happily obliterated Whitni's pinkness right then and there. "Break a leg," he grunted.

Whitni's round, rosy face crumpled and her little mouth sagged open. A gigantic wail burst forth and she ran from the room, patent-leather party shoes clattering. "Momma, Josh is being mean to me! He wants to break my leg!"

"Now look what you've done!" the Witch squawked at Josh from the downstairs hallway. "I just finished making up her face and you had to make her cry, and now her powder and blush are running all over! Can't you leave off tormenting these children for five minutes, Joshua? It's okay, honey muffin. Momma won't let bad big brother hurt you . . . "

Mercifully, the voice muffled into background noise as Mrs. Hickham and Whitni performed make-up repairs in the bathroom. Josh got up from his bed and padded across the room, his crew socks flopping on the wood floor. Before slamming the door he absorbed the ugliness of the hallway. The whole place, except for his room, was a nightmare of interior over-decoration. Ruffled curtains, doilies, flowered everything — it was like Whitni dressed for a baby beauty contest and transformed into a house.

Josh locked the door for good measure; now he was relatively safe from Kyler, the other midget monster. Sanctuary — that's what his bedroom was. The only part of the house not poisoned by the Witch's "taste," if you could call it that.

There was more yelling and then the Oldsmobile peeled out of the driveway, baby beauty contest-bound. The only noise now was the family room T.V., in front of which Kyler was probably planted, sitting too close with the volume too loud, hopefully melting his brain.

"Man, remind me never to have kids," Josh said out loud to himself. Though he supposed not all kids were Whitnis and Kylers. He himself had turned out semi-okay and so had his older brother, Jason.

What would Jason do if he were me? Josh wondered. Jason had lucked out. He graduated from high school and went into the Navy before the half-brats were old enough to wreak havoc, and before their dad totally opted out of family life and started leaving all the decisions up to his pushy young second wife.

Jason. Sometimes Josh missed his brother so much it hurt. He got an empty feeling somewhere around his stomach, the same as he got mid-afternoon when he'd skipped lunch.

Art store job's still open. That was the message T.J. had left on the dartboard at Split River Station, scribbled on a piece of notebook paper and stabbed through with a dart.

"Job's still open," Josh announced to the sketches and paintings wall-papering his room, trying to psyche himself up.

Jason would say do it, like T.J. Okay, I will! The phone was in the hall. Josh eased open his bedroom door. Good, Kyler was still downstairs basking in the rays of the boob tube. He picked up the receiver, even dialed a couple of digits. Then he chickened out, wimped, bit it. Pretended to himself he didn't remember the exact phone number, even though he had it memorized.

"You're worthless," he accused himself bitterly. He slammed back into his room. Dragging his feet, he slouched over to his desk. It was time to make excuses to himself: The job at Jake's was too good to lose 'cause of the free food. And what would Jake do without him? Josh was always willing to work extra shifts, the late-night ones nobody else wanted. He always needed the extra dough. Jake was a penny-pinching perfectionist and a real crab, but they got along.

Josh opened the top drawer of his desk. He pulled out a pad of sketching paper — almost out. And his last decent pen was starting to fuzz.

Light but firm, the fingers of his left hand grasped the pen, a black felt-tip. Without really thinking about it, he started doodling. Quick strokes, angling the pen to create thick or thin lines. The figures formed themselves almost magically.

Most of Josh's drawings told stories in a linear fashion, cartoon-style. But he didn't put bold black boxes around these characters. They all shared the same space, a whole sheet of off-white drawing paper.

Shaking his head, Josh snapped out of his daydream and focused on the drawing. Easy to give names to the people in it, and the setting.

Split River Station. A scrawny T.J. straddled a bike alongside a curvy Caroline. They were holding hands, but the Caro figure was half turned away, as distant as she was close. A bigger-than-life Marc Calamano gripped a football under one muscle-bound arm and a weighty volume of Shakespeare under the other while a wisp of an Alison danced along at his side. Darcy was pulled up in her new car but the doors were shut and the windows up and the Josh character looked like he wasn't sure he could count on a ride.

"Darcy." Josh whispered the name. Tasting it, trying to figure out its flavor. Why was she so hard to get to? *Or is it me?* he wondered.

The sketch spoke volumes. The BMW was sized way out of proportion and looked about as vulnerable as a tank. The Josh figure was small and puny in comparison. The Darcy in the drawing didn't need friends like Josh. "What do you want?" Josh asked the paper Darcy. Then he doodled a mustache on the drawing of himself. "What do *you* want?"

He didn't get a chance to answer his own question. Kyler started pounding with small, insistent fists on the bedroom door. Josh checked the clock radio. Sure enough, it was four, on the dot.

"Who taught the brat to tell time?" he muttered. A story and a snack . . . at least it'd give him an excuse to snarf a few cookies himself. Though with his luck, the Witch would count the contents of the cookie jar when she got home and get on his case about eating more than he paid for. And raise his rent.

"You're not cheering, Caro," T.J. observed, nudging her with his elbow.

"I'm not much of a football fan," she admitted, pushing a wind-tangled strand of hair from her face.

"It's easy," he assured her. "Doesn't take any particular talent or even knowledge of the sport. You just periodically yell a bunch of fairly pointless stuff. You know, like go team. Big D. First and ten, do it again. Kill 'em. Stuff like that."

Rubbing her hands together to warm them, Caroline smiled. "I'll give it a try," she promised T.J.

"All you gotta do is listen to the Calamanos. Yell whatever they yell," T.J. advised, lowering his voice.

Caro laughed. She, T.J., Darcy, and Mouse had met at the football game against West River High. Josh couldn't make it, being stuck at Jake's. The first

high-school football game Caro had ever attended —
it had been T.J.'s idea. None of them were your average Pep Club boosters, but Marc was playing. And
Marc's parents were sitting in the bleachers a couple
of rows away, cheering or cursing every single play.
They were so into it, it was amazing. Caro was sure
Mr. Calamano, a big Italian guy, was on the verge of
a coronary.

A football game . . . not the way Caroline Buchanan usually spent Friday nights. You didn't see
too many of the cool crowd hanging out in the
stands. *I could be somewhere else — I did get another offer . . .*

She held her bare hands to her mouth and blew on
them. *Stupid, not to bring gloves.*

T.J. saw her and took one of her hands in his,
briefly. "Ice," he observed. "I'll make a run to the
concession hut. Coffee?" Caro nodded. "How 'bout
you guys?"

Alison and Darcy decided on hot chocolate. T.J.
disappeared into the milling crowd of loud, partying
kids.

"What do you call that position Marc plays, anyway?" Caro asked Darcy, who was flipping through a
program.

"He's defense. Let's see . . . tight end, I think."

Caro's lips curved wickedly. "Tight end, huh? Always thought Marc had a nice one!"

Darcy put the program to her face to smother her
laughter.

"Especially in those stretchy pants," Caroline
added, making Darcy laugh louder. Caro looked at

Mouse. Definitely not tuned in to the joking. Instead Alison's attention was focused on the football field, of all places. Alison, who knew even less than Caro about sports and probably never watched a football game in her life, even on T.V.

Caro followed the track of her friend's intense gaze. She had a hunch. . . . Sure enough, Alison's wide brown eyes were glued on Number 18. Marc.

It was tempting to tease her, but Caro kept quiet. If something was happening between Mouse and Marc, it was something very new, very private, very delicate. *In other words, none of my business!*

With a start, Caro realized T.J. was staring up at her from the aisle, carefully balancing a cardboard box with four steaming cups. His watchful, penetrating look made her feel naked. She turned up the collar of her denim jacket. A moment later he slid onto the bench next to her. Wordlessly, Caro took the coffee he offered. She held the cup to her lips, warming the end of her nose in the steam.

"It's too damn cold to be sitting on our butts outside," T.J. observed, cautiously sipping his hot chocolate. "We could be *in*side, watching *Dallas* or something."

"You're the one who wanted to show your school spirit," Caro reminded him. "Don't blame me if your buns are frostbit."

T.J. gazed sideways at her, his eyes glinting green through the hot chocolate steam. Caro raised her eyebrows. "And don't look at me." Her low voice teased. "I'm not gonna warm 'em up!"

"My hopes are dashed," T.J. said lightly.

He was still looking at her, though, with those eyes that seemed to see straight into her soul. "I'm not going to be warming up anybody's buns," Caro added, on the defensive.

"Did I ask?"

"Maybe not in so many words." Caro turned her head away slightly. "I could have gone out with Brad tonight, you know."

"I know." T.J.'s voice was even.

"But I blew him off 'cause I already had plans. With you."

"You could've skipped the game. It's not a big deal. Marc probably doesn't even know we're here watching."

Shaking her head, Caro narrowed her eyes at T.J. He sounded so cool, so uncaring. Didn't he know she'd rather be with him than Brad, any time and under any circumstances? Maybe not. Well, she wasn't about to come right out and make an announcement during the halftime show. If he couldn't figure it out for himself . . .

"Not a big deal . . . " Was T.J. really that cool inside? Couldn't be. He had to feel like she did, making this kind of get-no-place-fast double talk — tense, shaky, lonely, dissatisfied.

"It's not too late, either," Caroline said, as if to herself but loud enough for T.J. to hear. It was true. Brad and a bunch of the guys were drinking beer at Joe's house tonight — she knew the address.

What a bitchy thing to do, she realized. Daring T.J. to tell her to go ahead, catch up with Brad. She swallowed a mouthful of coffee, waiting.

Tell me to get on out of here, then. Or ask me to stay with you, for the whole night. Stake your claim.

Predictably, T.J. did neither. He just slung an arm loosely around her cold, hunched shoulders, pointing out at the field with his half-empty Styrofoam cup. "Whatta pass, huh?"

A pass? You're sure not making one at me. "I think I missed it," Caro said with a wry smile.

"There'll be another one," T.J. promised meaningfully. "And if both players get it right . . ."

"What happens?"

"Touchdown!"

They both laughed. T.J. patted her shoulder and then started to remove his arm. Caroline put up a hand to hold it in place. "Just to stave off hypothermia," she assured him.

"Sure, go ahead and use me. T.J. McAllister, the human electric blanket . . ."

Snuggled under T.J.'s arm, Caro glanced at Alison and Darcy. Alison was still absorbed in Number 18's every movement. Even now when Marc was sucking Gatorade with a straw through the face guard of his helmet. A pretty sexy sight.

Darcy, meanwhile, sat with her arms and legs crossed. Against the cold maybe, or maybe against the whole scene, Caro speculated. It was typical high school, typical Redmond. Or rather typical of *her* part of town, not the Jenners' neighborhood. Kids drinking beers smuggled into the stands in their jacket pockets. Couples, not discouraged by the cold raw night air, sneaking off to the woods and underneath the bleachers. Working-class parents with Thermoses of spiked coffee, waving little maroon-and-gold pom-poms on sticks.

"Big D!" Caro hollered when Marc and the defensive squad trotted back out on the field.

Alison said nothing, just smiled softly, her cheeks glowing from excitement and the cold, as her eyes followed Number 18.

EIGHT

Saturday — a whole day, empty. With no school and no shift at Jake's, there was time and freedom for Josh to do anything he wanted. Do some sketching, maybe even try a watercolor . . .

Josh laughed at himself and his fantasy. He knew better. Saturday the Witch was in her element. She had him to boss around *and* his dad.

Already that morning Josh had washed windows and raked leaves. Now it was raining, steady slanting needles of ice water. More yardwork was out, but that didn't mean he was off the hook. Undoubtedly the Witch had a list as long as her arm of indoor chores.

The rain made a bike ride to Split River Station distinctly unappealing, though anything was better than submitting himself to torture at home. T.J.'s house was nearer and at least it'd be warm once he got there. And T.J.'s folks were cool — they said hi, friendly, and then let you alone.

Josh thumped down the stairs, sliding his arms into his jacket as he went. He crammed a baseball hat on his head to keep the rain out of his eyes while he biked. What luck. The Witch was on the phone, shouting over the roar of the dishwasher. He'd get away clean.

He slammed the front door, sucking in a mouthful of cold, damp pure air to wash out the taste of perfumey sachets the Witch planted all over the house. The rain was nasty — sideways and sharp, slicing into him like a scalpel. Once on his bike, he pedaled for all he was worth but he was still soaked to the skin by the time he reached Perry Street and the McAllisters'.

There was an unfamiliar Chevy pickup in the driveway — and a very familiar BMW. Josh coasted up on his bike, debating. He'd kind of been hoping for a quiet low-key type of scene, just him and T.J. But it was still a long way to the station and his fingers were starting to freeze on the handlebars. . . .

T.J. answered the doorbell. "Hickham!" he said with a wide smile. "Am I having a party I don't know about? Darcy and Marc are here, too. How'd everybody know my parents weren't gonna be around today?"

Josh shrugged out of his wet jacket. "Just a lucky guess. D'you mind?"

"You kidding?" T.J. punched him lightly on the arm. Water squelched from Josh's shirt. "Man, you're a sponge. You'll excuse me if I don't invite you to sit in

my dad's favorite armchair. Why don't you go upstairs and pick out something from the McAllister
wardrobe? We can stick your stuff in the dryer."

A few minutes later Josh presented himself sheep-
ishly in the cluttered living room, where Darcy and
Marc were slumped comfortably on the overstuffed
sofa. "My dream's finally come true," he joked. "I'm
T.J. McAllister."

Darcy's blue eyes crinkled. "Just be glad the attitude doesn't come with the clothes," she advised Josh.

T.J. raised a sardonic eyebrow at Darcy as he de-
posited a bowl of popcorn between her and Marc,
then dumped a couple of Cokes on the book-littered
coffee table. Josh sank into a smooshy chair, imagin-
ing how his stepmother would react to T.J.'s house.
Coffee-cup rings on the furniture, books and newspapers everywhere, dozens of family photographs in
plastic frames on the walls and shelves. It looked too
much like a *home* — the Witch would hate it.

Flipping channels on the T.V., T.J. searched for
some good reruns. Darcy and Marc resumed a conversation, Darcy first smiling at Josh in a way that invited him into it. "We had a riot at the game last night,
Marc. I didn't know you were such a star. It must be
fun to be so good at something, to play varsity and all.
Closest I ever got was alternate for the J.V. tennis
squad at Merton."

Marc lifted his shoulders, a massive movement like
a mountain shrugging. "It's not enough just to be good
at something. You oughta like it, you know?" he said,
reaching into the popcorn bowl with a giant fist.
"Football. Talk about an idiot game. I mean, you can

be smart about it. It takes some brains to be a good quarterback and all. But basically it's a bunch of big guys bashing each other, fighting over a stupid piece of pigskin and taking themselves completely seriously, like it really matters which team racks up more points."

Josh looked at Marc, unbelieving. *This* was the sports god talking?

Elbow on the couch arm, Darcy rested her head on her hand. "This is probably an incredibly dumb question, but if you feel that way . . . why do you play?"

Marc tipped back his head and chugged about half a can of Coke. *His neck's as big around as my leg,* Josh thought, awed.

"My family," Marc said simply. "You've got to understand — they live and die for football. My dad played ball in college and that was like the high point of his whole goddamn life. You know that Springsteen song, 'Glory Days'? That's my dad, talkin' about starting for Notre Dame in the sixties. Glory days. Both my brothers are doing it his way, in college on sports scholarships. And me, I got fed monster meals the whole time I was growing up. Not to make sure I was getting the eight important vitamins and minerals and stuff — just to make sure I'd get big enough to play football in high school."

Darcy laughed. "Looks like it worked."

"Yeah, it worked." Marc's smile was crooked. "I'm playing football. My folks are happy about it."

"I'd say," agreed Darcy wholeheartedly. "We saw them at the game — and heard them. Talk about busting a lung!"

Josh heard Marc's bitterness. "I'm glad at least *they're* enjoying themselves."

Darcy's smile softened, her eyes instantly sympathetic. "So you just do it for them?"

"They expect me to play." Marc shrugged carelessly. "It's easy, and it's not like there's anything else to do — at least in their eyes."

"I know," Darcy assured him, her vehemence taking Josh by surprise. "Believe me, I know. With me, it's not any one thing my parents expect. It's more general, like my whole life and personality basically. My parents have me slotted for this high-society assembly line." Her tone grew cynical. "Darcy the Debutante. She walks, talks, and never puts out on the first date."

One of Marc's brawny arms was stretched along the back of the sofa. He touched Darcy's shoulder. "Hope you don't mind my saying you don't *look* like a debutante."

She didn't, either. Josh's eyes wandered shyly over Darcy's neat form, curled on the couch. In tight torn jeans and a man's V-necked undershirt, she looked like anything but.

Darcy's eyes met Josh's briefly. Then she shrugged. "Maybe not on the outside. It's the inside that's harder to change." Her voice was quiet. "Sometimes I feel like I'm trying to climb out of this big pit. Getting lots of dirt under my fingernails, but not making much progress."

"It's a trap," Marc agreed. "Seems like everyone's got their own. Yours is playing socialite; mine just happens to be playing football. And the thing is —

let's face it — it's a stupid game. Every couple of weeks I get fed up and try to get kicked off the team. They're supposed to sack you if you make a C average or if you have some sort of academic problem. I've mouthed off to more teachers and failed more tests! But they always let me off the hook because I'm important to the team. I get in trouble, and the coach and the principal play 'Let's Make a Deal'."

Josh hadn't said a word, but his brain was soaking it all in. Listening to Marc talk about football, watching his face, it was very weird. Josh felt as if he knew Marc really well all of a sudden. He could sense that Marc was hiding something, heard what Marc wouldn't admit to Darcy — that there was some reason he wouldn't defy his family and the coach and just quit.

He's like me, sort of, Josh realized with a strangely painful but liberating insight. *I'm like his opposite. He doesn't have the guts to quit — I don't have the guts to get started, to come out in the open with my art.*

It made Josh want to laugh. He always thought guys like Marc Calamano had it made. Big man on campus, the superstar jock. Marc got his name in the local paper every week. Kids at school idolized him, and the prettiest girls threw themselves at his feet. Marc had this heroic he-man *aura*. Even Alison went for it. . . .

And Darcy. Josh'd never heard her talk about herself like that. Stepping outside of herself, opening up and revealing a new person. It was like suddenly there were two Darcys sitting on the couch, their outlines blurring. The high-class country club Darcy who was way out of his league, and another more down-to-earth Darcy.

Josh tentatively opened himself up to the atmosphere. Not that he was about to launch into *his* life story, but a couple of new feelings, new possibilities, sprouted inside him. Courage. Trust.

"That's my point!" T.J. exclaimed triumphantly. "Superman *is* sort of a modern Shakespearean hero. He has a dual self, you know? Part strong, part weak. And changing costumes and all, that's key — "

Marc threw a handful of popcorn at him. Darcy caught Josh's eye and twirled her index finger. "Loco," she said, indicating T.J.

"Bats," Josh agreed.

"I think this is my cue to take off." Darcy unfolded herself from the sofa. T.J. wasn't hinting anybody should leave, but she'd been there two hours. As she slipped her sweater on over her head Marc swatted her on the rear, locker-room style. Darcy socked him back and then shook her hand in mock agony. "Hard as a rock!" she joked.

Josh, stretching his arms over his head, looked like he was ready to make a move, too. Darcy saw him check out the view from the window. Outside it was prematurely dark and still pouring. He probably rode his bike, she speculated, spotting an opportunity. "Need a ride?" she offered hopefully.

"As a matter of fact — if you don't mind . . . "

"Of course not," Darcy assured him. "Your house is

on the way and we already know your bike fits in the trunk."

This time, tossing Josh's bike in the trunk of the BMW, Darcy didn't feel as awkward as she had the evening at the station. She knew Josh a little better than she did then. Buckling up in the front seat, though, she got the usual charge from his nearness. T.J.'s living room had been neutral territory — here in the car, she and Josh were alone, and close.

She watched him pull the seat belt around — his strong, supple hands, the roll of his shoulder muscles under his jacket — then looked quickly away the second *he* looked up at her.

"Marc's a nice guy, huh?" Darcy said to Josh, glad for the dim light to hide her blush.

Josh nodded. "You know, in all the years we've gone to the same schools I never really talked to the guy."

The BMW's wipers squeaked across the windshield as they headed away from Perry Street. Darcy glanced at Josh as she turned onto Main Street. "Funny how we give people a label, like 'jock,'" she agreed. "Then we assume the label says it all about that particular person."

She felt rather than saw that Josh was studying her, considering her tone and words. *Yeah, I'm talking about me, too,* she almost said.

"It's a two-way street, though," Josh pointed out. "Somebody like Marc . . . even if he's not wild about it and his parents pressure him, he still chose the crowd he's part of, the sports crowd. Labels aren't just what other people think about you. It's what you think about yourself. What you make yourself."

Josh's words hung in the air, practically visible, embedding themselves in Darcy's mind like darts on a dart board. Bull's-eye. *That's what it's all about*, she thought. *I'm trying to unmake myself. Remake myself.*

"Well, don't you think . . . " she began cautiously, like a person walking on the edge of quicksand, not sure where it was safe to place her foot. "Do you think people can change the direction they're going in? People like Marc." *Call a spade a spade, Jenner,* she commanded herself. "People like me," she added.

Now she glanced at Josh. His blue eyes were fixed on her, their expression frank. "The way I see it, people can do whatever the hell they want," he said simply, "if they've got the guts."

Darcy swerved onto Josh's road, nearly missing the turn. For once she felt like she and Josh were talking the same language. He was responding, not reacting, to her. It felt fantastic.

Damn. "Your house," she observed, her regret audible. She'd driven too fast; she should've dragged out the ride.

Pulling up alongside the curb opposite the Hickhams', she eased the stick into neutral.

For a long, silent moment Josh sat looking straight ahead, one hand on the door handle. Darcy's heart was jumping in time to the jerky rhythm of the windshield wipers. *Don't get your hopes up,* she counseled herself. *He's not about to ask you in.* Darcy knew better than to take it personally. Even though they'd never actually talked about the situation, the two of them, she understood Josh felt awkward about people coming over. Right now he seemed reluctant to leave her car and enter the house himself.

Suddenly Darcy became daring. A wave of spontaneity picked her up and swept her along. "Josh, um, I don't know if you have plans or anything right now," she began, talking fast so she couldn't wimp out. "But I was thinking about . . . how'd you like to go get dinner someplace?"

Josh basically gaped at her as if she'd suggested robbing a bank. *What'd I do wrong?* Darcy wondered. *Does he think I'm forward for asking him sort of on a date, or what?* Then, *Oh. Money. Obviously.*

He never had the spare cash to buy lunch at the school cafeteria, much less to throw away on dinner at a restaurant. Actually, she didn't have any money on her, either. But she had plastic. American Express, don't leave home without it.

"My treat," Darcy added casually, as if she'd intended to say it all along. Her eyes crinkled. "When my grandfather gave me the car, he also forked over some funds for gas. I'd rather eat than fill up the tank," she joked. "Join me?"

The pressure off, Josh relaxed, giving in to a grin. *He wants to be with me,* Darcy thought, delirious.

"Sure. I'm up for some chow," Josh said. "If Grandpa Jenner's footin' the bill!"

"All right!" Darcy exclaimed, shifting into first. *Warp factor three, full speed ahead.*

NINE

"So my brother, who's like ten, tells this baby-sitter who's at least a thousand years old that the insurance company's coming to inspect the chimney, and she has to get up on top of the house and sweep the roof before they get there."

Darcy put her elbows on the table and leaned forward. "She didn't fall for it."

Josh nodded. "Yeah, she did. This ancient lady was up on the roof sweeping off the leaves and stuff. Jason and I cracked up like you wouldn't believe. I thought we were gonna die laughing. Then my dad comes home from work and sees this woman up there like she thinks she's Santa Claus or something. He paddled our butts with a wooden spoon. But it was worth it."

It was fun to make Darcy laugh, Josh thought. Her eyes crinkled and her dimples made a smile out of her whole face. It was easy, too — she'd laugh at just about anything.

"I thought *I* was pretty hot when it came to practical jokes." Darcy shook her head, pushing a cherry tomato around on her salad plate with a fork. "I never did anything that wild, though! Jason sounds like a pretty decent person to have as a brother."

"He's a great brother." Josh dropped his eyes, not wanting to give too much away. "He's a great guy."

The waiter minced over to their table balancing a tray, and tenderly slipped a plate in front of Josh. Veal marsala and a side of linguini. Josh stared down at the food, inhaling the rich aroma of the sauce. Wine and mushrooms and fresh herbs . . . his stomach was begging for a bite. *Don't drool, bud. Or this'll be the last time Darcy Jenner asks you to dinner!*

How weird was it, anyway? Here he was, if you got right down to essentials, on his very first date with a girl. And *she'd* asked him. *She* was paying for him.

It figured he'd get it backwards. But Darcy was making it easy, making everything easy. Easy to talk to her and laugh with her and sit in the booth across from her. *Why was I ever scared of this girl?* he wondered.

Darcy had ordered pasta primavera. Now she speared a broccoli floweret, recalling, "I always wanted a brother. A big brother like Jason. Somebody to watch out for me, you know — and then when I got old enough, introduce me to all his good-looking friends!"

"You an only child?" Josh managed to ask in between mouthfuls.

"No — I have a sister. Sarah, she's in college. She's okay. But we're not *friends* like you and Jason are. I could never tell her stuff. She's like a clone of my mother. Always the perfect kid. Did everything my parents wanted her to."

"Grim." Josh buttered another slice of Italian bread, about his tenth — he'd lost count. "But you don't have to follow in her footsteps."

"No, I don't suppose I do." Darcy rolled some fettucine onto her fork. "You planning to follow in Jason's footsteps?"

"Sure. I'm splitting Redmond the minute I graduate."

"Not even going to take the time to change out of your cap and gown?" Darcy teased.

Josh laughed. "I'll show up in it at Navy boot camp."

The second he said it, Josh wished he hadn't. He'd mentioned the Navy once to T.J., and T.J. had practically bitten his head off. Darcy was even less likely than T.J. to understand that Josh didn't have all the options in the world. Expensive private colleges all over the U.S. were dying to open their doors to kids like Darcy Jenner, not to kids like him.

But Darcy didn't ask nosy questions or pass any kind of judgment. "Your brother's in the Navy, huh?" she said instead.

An awkward moment avoided, Josh told Darcy about Jason's latest assignment in the Middle East, experiencing a funny sensation of watching himself talk. He sounded like somebody else, a stranger. Josh Hickham was usually tongue-tied with girls, but not this guy. He might not be as glib as T.J., but he was holding his own.

Darcy listened attentively, now and then nodding with a little half-smile. *She's really pretty*, Josh realized. He felt light-headed, a little bit drunk even though they were having club soda because Darcy got carded when she tried to order a bottle of wine. He had an urge to laugh out loud, high-five the waiter. *This is me, actually sharing a secluded candlelit booth at Giapetto's with this gorgeous girl.* And Giapetto's wasn't your average take-out joint; the linen tablecloth alone probably cost as much as he got paid in a week.

"You've got to have dessert," Darcy insisted as the waiter whisked away their dinner plates. "Last time I was here I had this chocolate fudge cake thing with like, a sundae on top. It was awesome."

Josh scanned the dessert menu, feeling happy and well-fed. *A square meal for once. This is the way to live.*

When the check came on a little black tray, Darcy took it calmly and gave it a quick once-over. Then she conjured a charge card from her wallet, placing it on the tray with a snap of plastic.

Josh felt suddenly inadequate, a low-life slouch compared to Darcy. Her self-assurance as she whipped out her credit card . . . She looked like one of those T.V. commercials where at the end they type the owner's name out on the card, and it turns out to be somebody famous. Even in a T-shirt, Darcy had the look, the moves.

She caught him staring and lifted her shoulders

helplessly, blushing slightly. "What can I say? It's the only way I ever pay," she confessed. "Saves fussing with my parents over a weekly allowance and stuff."

A few minutes after the waiter trotted off with the little tray and Darcy's charge card, he reappeared, apologizing. "I'm sorry, Miss Jenner. But I'm afraid the charge was declined. If you'd like to pay with another card — "

Josh watched Darcy's face, fascinated. The warm softness of her eyes dissolved and her expression iced up like winter's first frost. *Nobody says "no" to Darcy Jenner,* Josh surmised.

"No, I would not like to pay with another card," Darcy informed the waiter smoothly. "Please try this one again. It looks like there's been a mistake."

Impressive. She had to be at least a little embarrassed but you'd never know it.

The waiter bustled away again and Darcy shrugged, unworried. "This sort of thing happens all the time," she explained in a worldly tone. "Once I was at this boutique near Merton — it was spring and I was in the mood for new rags, you know? So, I picked out about fifty different things, and the girl at the counter painstakingly wrote out every single one of them on the slip and figured the tax and everything. The charge didn't go through the first time — I thought she was going to hit the ceiling. She was steaming, 'cause obviously I didn't have a few hundred dollars in cash on me! But then she called again and that time — "

The waiter was back, his apologetic look even more pronounced. "I'm sorry," he said again, depositing the tray with the credit card. "We cannot accept your charge. Would you like to pay cash?"

As Josh watched, wondering what her next move was going to be, two spots of bright color sprang up in Darcy's cheeks. She reached for her water glass and took a fast sip. "Um, yes. We'll pay cash," she said, her voice trembling ever so slightly. "Could you come back in a few minutes?"

The waiter melted obligingly away, leaving Josh and Darcy facing one another across the table. A few minutes? Josh's mouth went dry. Darcy's wallet was right there on her lap — either she had the money . . . or she didn't.

"I don't understand," Darcy said. The spots on her cheeks had spread, washing her whole face scarlet. "My father's secretary pays my charge-card bills out of the family account. I don't know . . . maybe he got behind mailing out the checks or something." Mortification had nearly robbed Darcy of her voice, but she appeared determined not to break down. "And I don't have any cash on me," she said, somehow still managing to sound casual, as if it were no big deal. "Josh, do you have any money?"

Josh's stomach gave a sickening lurch. He looked at Darcy's cool high-society smile. Some nameless Jenner employee screwed up, and here's the rich girl, treating it like it's some sort of game.

And now I'm getting stuck with the bill. Josh swallowed, putting a hand to his back pocket to touch his wallet. Luckily it wasn't empty, for once — he'd cashed his paycheck that morning. But it was money he needed to pay his stepmother rent.

"What the hell?" he blurted out, his face darkening, furious. Furious at her and equally furious at himself — just moments ago he'd been savoring the great Jenner aura. *She's a fake*, he thought, *just like her whole high-society scene. I hate the way my step-mother idolizes those people, and here I am, doing the same thing.*

"I'm sorry," Darcy croaked. "I had no idea this was going to happen — "

"Oh, c'mon. It's your own credit card. You mean, you don't know if the bill's been paid or not?"

"No, I don't know if the bill's been paid or not," Darcy snapped back. "Because I don't pay it. I just—"

"You just spend it," Josh finished for her.

"Something like that," she said, her tone brittle.

Josh stared at Darcy. All of a sudden she didn't seem pretty to him anymore. She looked smooth and cold and unreal. Plastic, like a doll or like that charge card. That round innocent face, those baby-blue eyes . . . It hit him like an avalanche. *She's a grown-up Whitni. A great big spoiled brat.* Josh laughed, the sound bitter and hollow. "It's a good trick, Darce. Gotta get me a credit card and try it some time."

"It's no trick. God!" Darcy exclaimed, pounding on the table. The silverware jumped. "I never in a million years thought they'd reject the charge. What do you think I am? The only reason I offered to pay for dinner in the first place was because I felt sorry for you!"

"Felt sorry for you . . . " The terrible words seemed to echo through the restaurant. Darcy's face went pale and she put her hand to her mouth.

Josh gripped the edge of the table, his knuckles whitening. "I didn't ask for your pity. In fact, I'm not the one who asked *you* out tonight," he said, his voice hoarse. "Why the hell don't you stay where you belong, with your own goddamn kind?"

Tears sparkled in Darcy's shocked eyes. "Josh, I — "

He stood up abruptly, knocking over a water glass. Fumbling in his wallet, he threw down five ten-dollar bills. Then he bolted.

Darcy sat stiff and frozen in the booth. She stared at the fifty dollars and then looked up, catching a glimpse of Josh's departing back.

Not caring what the waiter thought as he silently took the money, Darcy bent the card until it snapped in two. What a stupid thing to depend on! She'd been dumb enough to imagine it could smooth things out, make a fun evening for her and Josh. Instead it'd ruined everything. Forget a friendship with Josh, ever — she'd just killed any chance for one.

" . . . *Why don't you stay where you belong?*" As Darcy hurried across the restaurant parking lot in the rain, Josh's angry words repeated insistently in her head like a record album on a skip. He'd really said it, spelled it right out. *What* am *I doing, trying to fit in with someone like him?* And now he'd disappeared into the rainy night. He didn't even have his bike, which was still locked in Darcy's trunk.

Damn you, Josh Hickham! Darcy cursed silently. But she knew inside that the problem wasn't with

Josh. She gunned the engine of the BMW and yanked the car onto Oak Boulevard. The problem was with her and her stupid mixed-up, misguided attitudes.

Furious, Darcy kept her foot heavy on the gas, bumper-riding the car in front of her. *It's my family's fault. Every single Jenner, all the way back to the goddamn Mayflower. Everything's their fault!* It made sense to Darcy, blaming them. Ever since she was a toddler, she'd been led to believe she could have anything she wanted, just like magic. Or rather, just like money. Ask and you shall receive. Fork out the dough and it's yours.

My family's fault, Darcy repeated to herself. If Grandpa Jenner hadn't given her the BMW and her father hadn't given her the credit card, she wouldn't have tried to act like a big shot and take Josh out to dinner. Everything was falling apart and it was their fault, their fault she didn't fit in.

High Ridge Road was empty and dark. Dying leaves, ripped off the maple trees by the rain, slapped against the windshield. Darcy passed the Rhiner estate, double-taking at the dozens of cars parked along the driveway. *That's right — Sue's home for the weekend and throwing a party.* She'd been invited, of course, but up until this moment she'd forgotten all about it.

She could stop by. . . . There'd probably be lots of people there she hadn't seen since she left Merton. *My kind, like Josh said. Where I belong.*

Darcy kept on driving.

The Jenner house was lit warmly against the wet night like a gray stone jack-o-lantern. Darcy coasted the BMW into the barn-sized garage. Before killing the lights and the engine she took a look at herself in the rearview mirror. Damp and crumpled hair, tear-stained cheeks. And the way her lips were pursed and her jaw set stubbornly, she looked exactly like her mother when she was mad. *Scary.*

The big house was quiet and drafty. Padding down the hall in her sneakers Darcy felt like a burglar, a trespasser.

She found her parents in the library. A fire crackled in the fireplace, its light sparkling on their brandy snifters, and classical music wafted from invisible speakers. A peaceful, hateful scene. Darcy wished the room and everything in it were made of glass so she could smash it, break it into a million priceless pieces.

"Darcy, where have you been?" Mrs. Jenner asked, her tone a mixture of anger and relief.

At the same moment, her father caught sight of the expression on Darcy's face. "Honey, is something the matter?"

Darcy felt the tears starting again and bit her lip, hard. She didn't want to bawl like a child — she wanted to scream. "Yes, something's the matter," she burst out. "I've just had the worst night of my life, if you want to know. I tried to go out to dinner with a friend at Giapetto's, and they wouldn't take my credit card and so he had to pay and . . . " Even to her own ears, she sounded feeble and whiny. *That's not what I wanted to say*, she realized. *That's not really what's the matter.*

"Your American Express card?" Mr. Jenner ran a vague hand through his faded, thinning hair and glanced at his wife. "There must have been some mistake."

"No mistake, Daddy," Darcy said flatly. Suddenly she thought of the country club and the liquor store. Was there a pattern here? "It's because the bill hasn't been paid, isn't it?" she guessed.

"Well, let's see," her father said vaguely. "Maybe Robert mislaid the statement, or forgot to mail the check."

"Maybe Robert *forgot* to mail the check for a couple months now," Darcy suggested sarcastically. "Why don't you tell me the truth?"

Then a new, horrible possibility occurred to her. *What if they didn't pay my bill on purpose? It's just another slap in the face, another way of punishing me for misbehaving at Merton and disgracing the family name. They're going to make me suffer for it for the rest of my life.* The tears Darcy had been trying so hard to restrain suddenly were there, running down her cheeks and making her mouth tremble so badly she could barely talk.

"I know why this happened," she said, her voice high and jerky with sobs. "It's punishment, just like sending me to public school's supposed to be."

"Honey, no." Mrs. Jenner rose from her chair, her forehead creased with distress. "We would never — "

"Yes, you would!" Darcy cut in, wiping quickly at her burning eyes. "But I don't care any more. You can punish me all you want. It's not going to work because I don't need your charge cards, and I'm doing just fine at Norwell High. I wouldn't go back to Merton for my goddamn life."

The cool look of disapproval had returned to Mrs. Jenner's face while Darcy made this speech. "Darcy, I don't like your tone," she said.

"You don't? Am I talking too plain for you, Mom? That's right, I forgot. Nobody talks straight in this family."

"All right, Darcy, if you want to talk straight you can tell us where you've been for the past six hours," her mother rejoined. "Didn't it occur to you we might be worried?"

"You're changing the subject," Darcy accused. "You're doing what you always do, turning things around so you can blame me."

"I'd like an answer to my question, not smart talk," Mrs. Jenner snapped.

"I was hanging out with some people, okay?" Darcy said, hating the fact that she was on the defensive once again. "Some guys from Norwell. Are you satisfied?" she added, knowing her mother wouldn't be.

"No, I'm not satisfied," Mrs. Jenner declared, predictably. "I'll tell you the truth, since you seem to want me to speak plainly. I don't like you running around town for hours on end with no particular destination, and spending all your time with people we know nothing about."

Mr. Jenner put a placating hand on Darcy's arm. "Darcy, honey, we just worry about you. We know it hasn't been easy for you leaving Merton and attending public school, but being at Norwell doesn't change who you are. You're still a Jenner. And it might be for the best if you didn't see so much of these kids outside of school hours."

Darcy shook off her father's hand. "You can't make my friends for me any more, Daddy. You can't tell me who to be. I won't stop seeing my new friends. They happen to be the first real people I've ever known."

Her parents just stared at her, shaking their heads. Darcy felt like she'd been shouting at them through a glass wall. They just didn't hear her; they didn't hear anything they didn't want to. She couldn't change their opinions, make them see that *she* was changing when their minds were as fixed as cement. They could never understand what she was feeling.

"You know what I think about your ideas about what's right and what's wrong?" Darcy asked her parents, her voice cracking with emotion. "They're a prison. And you don't even know enough to realize you're prisoners." She spun around and ran from the room.

TEN

"Happy birthday to you, happy birthday to you," Caro sang tunelessly, ripping the pages from another comic book. "Happy birthday, Clark Kent and Lois with the idiotic spike heels, happy birthday to you."

T.J.'s going to croak, she thought happily as she taped the pages to the station wall, which was already half-papered with *Superman* comics. It was his birthday and they were all pitching in — Josh was home drawing a homemade birthday card and Darcy had said she could get the cook at her house to bake a cake. Caroline had bought balloons and streamers and the drugstore's whole inventory of *Supermans*. Split River Station was starting to look like New Year's eve.

She'd been tearing and taping for an hour, but it'd be worth it to see T.J.'s face when he walked in later. "Anyhow I owe him one," she reminded Superman and herself.

T.J. would never admit his feelings were hurt because she'd been seeing Brad occasionally. He respected her freedom and all that. But Caro knew her own attitude was definitely a little bogus. Sure, she liked Brad, but rubbing it in T.J.'s face made it a head game, and she'd always detested people who played games.

So why can't I stop playing this one? she wondered. *Why do I need the sort of attention I get from guys like Brad?* Good questions — the kind that didn't come with answers attached. Caro shook them out of her head with a toss of her hair.

T.J. knows I don't mean it, anyway, she thought, settling down on the cock-eyed sofa to read a comic before ripping it up. *He knows with Brad it's just passing time.*

Just then the station door made the belching sound that usually meant someone was trying to unwedge it and come in.

It can't be T.J. It better not be!

It was.

"Go away! Close your eyes!" Caro shouted, flinging the comic book aside and jumping up, as if she could really hide all those balloons and streamers.

"Hey, it's a party," T.J. observed. "Am I late?"

Caro gave in and laughed. "No, you're early, you bum! Go back outside and come in again."

Grinning, T.J. did. This time when he opened the door she yelled, "Surprise!"

T.J. put his hands to his face. "Knock me over with a feather," he declared. "A surprise party for *me?* You shouldn't have!"

"Shut up, McAllister," Caro said affectionately. "What are you doing here anyway? Darcy swore on the Jenner family Bible you two were going to have to stay after school till all hours working on your chem-class project. I thought my secret was safe."

"We just got started and Darce dropped our beaker," T.J. explained. "We have to start over from scratch in lab tomorrow. So it was such a great day, I went for a marathon bike ride, all the way up to South Chester. Stopped off here to catch my breath."

T.J. crossed the room. "Hey, look at this! Genuine Superman wallpaper. Always wanted something like this in my bedroom, you know? And sheets and stuff to match."

Caroline smiled, pleased. "Knew you'd like it," she said smugly.

He slipped an arm around her waist and kissed her. On the cheek, a fast one. "I love it. This is a great surprise party. Thanks," he said, his green eyes warm and serious.

Pretending she wanted to adjust a drooping streamer, Caro stepped away. "Well, the real party's later. You could call this a sneak preview. So tonight, act like you're totally shocked and thrilled and all that, okay?"

T.J. flopped onto the sofa. "Will do. Who's attending my birthday bash, anyway?"

Caroline knelt on the other end of the couch, mischievous. "The place'll be packed to the rafters. Probably be a whole half dozen people here. Just us. Just who knows about the place — Darce, Mouse, Josh, and Marc."

"Darcy and Josh in the same room?" T.J. wrinkled his forehead. "Didn't know they'd kissed and made up."

"I don't think they have," Caro admitted. In fact, Darcy had told her just that afternoon at school that Josh was still avoiding her. "But this is as good a time as any. They both know the other one will be here. And Darcy's been lookin' for a chance to talk to Josh. Apologize."

T.J.'s eyes narrowed thoughtfully. "Josh never did mention what happened, being his usual talkative self. Darcy was the one that told me."

"Me, too." Caro recalled the conversation, one recent morning before school, out back at the smoking lounge for privacy. Even though Darcy'd been on the edge of tears the whole time, she never lost that proud, private look. She hadn't been looking for sympathy. Just advice.

"You think Josh'll be okay about it?" Caro asked.

T.J. shrugged. "It's not like Darce did anything to him, committed a crime. They had a major misunderstanding. It's a two-way street."

"What Darcy said to him, though. About feeling sorry for him. That was pretty low. I couldn't believe it when she told me. If I were him, I'd've thrown something at her."

"Yeah, but think about it. You and me, sometimes *we* feel sorry for the guy. His home life rots. He doesn't eat lunch. Right? We just haven't slipped up and come right out and screamed it at him."

T.J. had a point, and Caro knew Darcy had been hurt, too, by Josh. "It's pretty easy to say something

you don't mean," she observed. "Then you'd do anything to take it back, but you can't."

"And let's face it. Darcy and Josh are really different. And they know it."

Caro sat back, putting her feet on the couch and
lining them up with T.J.'s, her boot soles pressed
against the bottoms of his sneakers. "Do you think
they're too different?"

T.J. considered. "No," he decided. "Nobody's too
different to understand another person. But they both
have to work at finding common ground. It can't be
all Darcy or all Josh. The two-way thing again."

"Darcy wants to get there." Caroline spoke slowly,
looking for the words to describe what she thought
Darcy was going through. "Remember the first day of
school, when she'd just transferred from boarding
school and all?"

T.J. raised one eyebrow. "Yeah, like I might ever
forget that day!"

Caroline tipped back her head, laughing. "That's
right. It was about as much fun for you as for her. But
I'm talking about the way she looked and everything.
My point is, I think she's trying to change."

But even as she said that Caroline wasn't sure she
was totally on target. She still wasn't sure she *knew*
Darcy. Thinking about it now, she realized Darcy
wasn't hanging around the station as much lately.
She'd only been by once since her disaster dinner with
Josh, to drop off his bike and an envelope containing
the money she owed him.

"People aren't like houses," T.J. pointed out. "They
can't just redecorate themselves."

But they can *change*, Caro thought, dropping her eyes. She should know. She changed after she met T.J. Not on purpose — it just happened, in the course of things.

"Well, do you suppose we can do anything to help them out?" she asked.

"You've already done it. They'll see each other tonight and they'll have to break the ice somehow."

While they were talking, the afternoon had faded into sunset. The light coming through the one window in the station that wasn't boarded up was warm and golden. Without really thinking about it, Caro shifted her position on the sofa so that she was sitting in the crook of T.J.'s arm, her head resting on his chest. "Speaking of happy couples, what do you think's going on with Marc and Mouse?"

"I dunno, you tell me," T.J. rejoined. "You know them better than I do."

"Well, I know Mouse at least," Caroline agreed. "And I know that for an art type she's all of a sudden a big football fan."

T.J. laughed, the amusement vibrating from his body right into hers. "And Marc's thinking of auditioning for the next school play, eh?"

Caro smiled, rubbing her cheek against the soft flannel of T.J.'s shirt. "I think it's one of those chemical reaction things."

"Hmmm." T.J. twined his fingers in a strand of her long hair. "Kinda like us, huh?"

"Kinda." *You know it, McAllister*, Caro added silently. *And here we are, as usual, talking about everything and everyone but us.* It was definitely the pattern lately. Sure, they'd promised to always be honest with one another, but being honest didn't necessarily mean sharing every thought. These days Caroline's main unconfessed thought was that it was hard to be friends with someone you thought you might be in love with.

Dusk had brought a chill to the station. Involuntarily, T.J.'s arms tightened around Caroline. She lifted her face. As their eyes met she caught her breath. The recognition that passed between them . . . it was like a discovery made in a dream, like figuring out the answer to a riddle you've already solved on some other deeper level.

When T.J. kissed her, Caro responded with all the need and desire she'd been harboring since their last kiss, their first kiss.

Then she pulled herself back from the edge, focusing on T.J. through the sharp blur of sensation. She wanted to burn right along with the fire. She was ready. But the time had to be right for him, too.

"I thought you just wanted to be friends," she reminded him, teasing and dead-serious at the same time.

"I'm tired of being friends," T.J. said huskily.

"That's funny," Caro whispered. "Me, too."

T.J. snapped awake from a light doze. His left arm was asleep and felt like some foreign object attached to his body. He shifted it underneath Caro's shoulders, careful not to wake her up.

Then he closed his eyes again, reveling in his latest,

most magical memory. It'd been hard to stop where
they did. He hadn't wanted to. But Caro had remembered that Josh or Darcy might come by the station to
help her get things organized. When you make love
with someone for the first time you don't exactly want
one of your buddies walking in on you. So they'd
satisfied themselves with kissing and touching and
then let the warm closeness pull them into a nap.

Gently, T.J. brushed the hair from Caro's forehead.
With her eyes closed and her face quiet she looked like
a different person. Younger, less complicated. The
moods that skittered elusively over her face like cloud
shadows on a windy day were under wraps. When
she was asleep he couldn't read her feelings in her
eyes.

You're just a kid, T.J. realized, tracing Caroline's
cheekbones with a feather-light finger. *God, I'm
crazy about you.*

It was hard to lie still. T.J. felt like he was spinning,
like he was on one of those amusement-park rides
where the floor drops out and you're suspended in air,
weightless.

Bending his head, he put his lips on Caro's, kissing
her gently. Her eyes popped open.

"Prince Charming, at your service," T.J. joked, suddenly feeling shy, on trial. Alone, with Caro sleeping,
he could believe anything he wanted. She was his.
Caro plus T.J., true love 4-ever and all that. Awake,
no matter how close their bodies were, she became
separate again.

Caro smiled up at him, her eyelids sleep-heavy.
"You don't *look* like a prince," she teased. "You look

like a scruffy high-school kid who just got his socks knocked off in an old railway station."

T.J. laughed. "Yeah, well it's the style these days. We princes do a lot of undercover work. I assure you, though, you've got the genuine article."

"Prince Charming, huh?" Caroline slipped her arms around T.J.'s neck. "Well, this must be my lucky day. Always wanted to meet the guy."

For a moment they lay in each other's arms, silent and relaxed. *Peace — this is it*, T.J. thought.

Then Caro spoke softly, her breath warm against his neck. "We broke our resolution, McAllister. We weren't acting like friends a while ago, d'you think?"

T.J. buried his face in her long, silky hair. "No, I'd say 'friends' doesn't quite describe it. Definitely inadequate. We need a new word, I'd say."

"So what'll it be?" Caroline pushed him gently away from her so she could see his face. "What are we going to call ourselves now?"

They couldn't go back; Caro's eyes said as much and T.J. knew it himself. When he hesitated, she spoke again. "It wasn't really working anyhow, was it? Outside I was your friend, but inside . . . And the whole casual thing. Dating other guys. That wasn't working for me, either."

It's like a chess game, T.J. thought. *If only I could figure out the right move . . .*

"Do you want to be my boyfriend?" Caro asked. Then she laughed at herself. "God, I feel like I'm in junior high. Some sophisticated proposal, huh?"

Caroline Buchanan's boyfriend — do I want it? Dumb question! But even as he got ready to sprint for paradise, T.J. remembered Leon. Leon Fiero had been Caro's "boyfriend" without ever really touching her soul. That wouldn't be enough. That couldn't be him.

"Well, I think we're running up against another question of definition," T.J. suggested. "What's a boyfriend exactly?"

He studied Caro's face as she considered. Her changeable green eyes clouded to ocean-grey. Happiness moved over and made room for uncertainty. "I don't know," she confessed.

ELEVEN

"Y'know, Darce, I think we went wrong somewhere." T.J. waved a hand in front of his face and gagged. "It's a smoke-out!"

And what a *smell*. Darcy pinched her nose shut with her right thumb and index finger. Her voice came out nasal. "The book says when we mix the white powder with the blue liquid we're supposed to get a bubbling green liquid." She couldn't even see through the small cloud they'd created. "What'd we get?"

"We got a mucous-yellow liquid and a fart-brown gas!" T.J. gasped. "Let's evacuate!"

Darcy burst out laughing and then accidentally inhaled a lungful of the stuff. "Here comes Mr. Macy," she choked out between coughs. "Try to look like we planned it this way!"

The chemistry teacher flicked on the fan over their

lab station. Miraculously, the ceiling sucked up the brown cloud.

Mr. Macy's smooth egg-shaped face was puckered like he'd just eaten something that tasted the way Darcy's and T.J.'s experiment smelled. "For your information, Mr. McAllister and Miss Jenner, the rest of the class is on step five of this experiment. If my eyes and my nose don't deceive me, you have yet to successfully complete step one."

Darcy smiled angelically. T.J. looked proud of this accomplishment. Mr. Macy's expression soured even further. "I would *suggest*," he continued in a sarcastic drone, "if you don't want to get an F-minus on this lab, that you stay after school again today. And get it right this time, please."

The instant Mr. Macy turned his back, Darcy pruned her face into a fair imitation of his teacherly scowl. "I would *suggest*, Mr. McAllister," she hissed, giggling wickedly, "that Mr. Macy drinks stuff like this for breakfast."

T.J. stirred the yellow gook with an evil grin. "It's a Jekyll and Hyde thing," he whispered back. "He's a decent guy when he wakes up in the morning, good-looking even. Then he whips up a glass of the ol' white powder and blue liquid. Downs it in one swallow. And poof!"

Darcy walked over to the supply cabinet and returned with a clean beaker. "You measure this time. I don't trust myself."

They both held their breath as T.J. added the blue liquid to the white powder and the mixture turned a startling shade of green. "We did it!" T.J. exclaimed triumphantly. "We're stars! I predict a Nobel prize in chemistry for this day's work."

"Don't get cocky," Darcy warned. "We've still got four steps to go."

Step two was easy: add another kind of powder to the green liquid and wait ten minutes. Darcy and T.J. slumped onto lab stools and stared lazily at their beaker.

"How'd you know chocolate's my favorite?" T.J. asked out of nowhere.

"Hmm?"

"Last night, at the party. My birthday cake!"

Darcy twirled on her stool. "Chocolate is *everybody's* favorite."

T.J. looked hurt. "I thought you made it special."

She laughed. "I didn't make it at all! Colleen made it. Our cook," she added and then wished she hadn't. It sounded so pompous. *Our cook. No kidding!*

"Well, whatever. It was a great cake." T.J. puffed out his cheeks. "I ate two more pieces at home before I went to bed."

"Glad you liked it."

T.J. lapsed into a daydream and Darcy did likewise. She bet they were both thinking about his birthday party the night before, but for different reasons.

Thinking Caroline might need a hand blowing up balloons, Darcy and her chocolate cake had arrived at the station a little early. She'd opened the door to find Caro and the birthday boy himself. T.J. and Caro had bounced up from the couch rumpled and with silly grins, and they'd acted drunk the whole night.

At least somebody had a good time, Darcy mused

bitterly. She wished she'd been drunk for real. It would have been easier to talk to Josh that way.

Just remembering their awful, awkward conversation made Darcy flush. She ducked her head, hiding her face from T.J. behind a curtain of hair.

She'd agonized so much about what to say beforehand that when the encounter actually took place she sounded like a pre-recorded announcement. "I didn't mean what I said the other night at the Italian restaurant. I was upset and it came out wrong. We were having such a good time. I hope you'll give me another chance," etc., etc.

Josh had listened politely, registering about as much emotion as if Darcy were asking if he preferred Coke or Pepsi. Then he'd shrugged and mumbled, "It's okay. Let's forget about it." And walked away.

Not that there'd been any place to go. The station was small and there were only six people there, after all. But she and Josh might as well have been at opposite ends of an empty football stadium. You could practically touch the chilly space stretching between them. Josh had forgiven her on the surface because he had to, it being T.J.'s birthday party and all, but underneath he hadn't come close to defrosting. And Darcy hadn't been able to tell what kind of vibes she was getting from the others. Whose side were they on? If they had to pick, Josh's probably. She'd left the party early.

"Step two, check it out." T.J. held up the beaker for Darcy's inspection. "A greyish sediment just like the book says. Don't you wish life worked out this neat and easy?"

"Do I," Darcy muttered, snapping the tip off her pencil as she went to record the results in their lab notebook.

Her thoughts went back to the subject of T.J. and Caro. If they *had* attained higher love, you wouldn't have known it to watch them together during lunch in the cafeteria last period. They exchanged private-joke type smiles all the time, but there was still some kind of distance between them. And then Caro had suggested a night on the town, meaning her, Darcy, and the BMW — no T.J. — just as if nothing had changed.

Darcy was mystified. But at this point she knew better than to ask Caro too many questions. She'd get the scoop by and by, maybe.

Darcy snuck out of the house at eight after lying to her parents about going to a movie with Sue. *What a wimp*, she thought, disgusted with herself. She hadn't planned to lie, it had just come out that way, as if somebody else were talking. And her parents ate it right up, patting her on the shoulder with pleased smiles. How nice that Darcy was spending so much time with Sue lately. See, dear? It's easy to stay in touch with your old friends, and so on. If they only knew the truth!

Caro must have been waiting in the lobby of her apartment building because she hit the sidewalk the second Darcy honked. She was wearing the usual tight jeans, T-shirt, and boots but no jacket — the night was balmy and springlike.

"Hey," Darcy greeted her, leaning over to open the passenger side door. "Hop in the Cruisemobile."

"Not a minute too soon," Caro said as Darcy pulled out from the curb. "My Dad got Suzi a new toy. A camcorder. Home movies, you know? They actually thought I might like to hang around and take pictures of them, probably slobbering all over each other." Caroline flipped down the visor and eyed her reflection, combing her hair with her fingers. "I'm sure they'll have more fun without me," she added.

Darcy shuddered. Her own parents were no prize, but Caroline's father sounded like a nightmare. Darcy couldn't blame her for escaping every chance she got.

They reached an intersection. "Nordecke Street?" Darcy asked.

"Where else?"

Friday night — the strip was crawling with cars. Darcy joined the parade, feeling like she'd driven into a song from Bruce Springsteen's early years. Groups of guys lounged on street corners, their paychecks cashed and burning holes in their pockets, scoping tribes of girls with fluffy hair and stiletto heels. The hole-in-the-wall bars were already packed, windows steaming up, beer lights blinking. There was music everywhere, stealing out of the bars and the cars.

Darcy dreaded Caro suggesting they leave the security of the BMW, but she wanted to seem up for adventure. Swallowing her cowardice, she stuttered, "Um, you want to go in someplace?"

"You got I.D.?" Caroline asked bluntly.

Darcy blushed. "Uh, no, actually I don't," she admitted.

Caro's smile was tolerant. "I'd rather drive anyway."

"Me, too," said Darcy, relieved. "Hey, isn't that Brad's truck?" The blue Ford was parked in front of McSweeney's Pub.

Slouching comfortably in the passenger seat, Caro nodded. "Um-hmm."

"Well . . . you want to hook up with him?"

A careless shrug. "Not really."

"Oh." Darcy waited, hoping for more, but Caro didn't satisfy her curiosity.

At the next stoplight, Caro reached over and shook Darcy's shoulder. "Darce, check this guy out," she urged in an admiring whisper. "Is he James Dean reincarnated or what?"

Darcy leaned forward to look past Caroline. Pulled up alongside them, its engine idling with an urgent rumble, was a vintage Camaro. As Darcy gaped at the driver's chiseled profile he turned slowly and stared right into her eyes. Darcy sat back quickly.

The guy smiled, his dark deep-set eyes narrowed against the smoke from his cigarette. Almost against her will, Darcy found her gaze pulled back in his direction.

He looked older, or maybe it was just the six o'clock shadow. Caro was right — he did look like James Dean, or the Marlboro man without the cowboy hat.

Suddenly Darcy got a funny, sure feeling in her gut. He was a badlander, a guy from the seedy side of town, the seen-better-days part she drove through to get to Split River Station.

Caroline's window was down. The guy's, too. After

checking out the two of them for a leisurely moment, he flicked his burnt-down butt onto the pavement. "You know Sand Hill, off Cross County Road?" The voice was deep and gravelly. Sexy. A hot-cold flicker shot up Darcy's spine like lightning. What was he going to propose?

"Sure," Caro answered him.

He shook another cigarette out of a crushed pack. "I'm headin' out there, the dead end. Party with some of my friends. If you're lookin' for something to do . . ." His words trailed off but his piercing gaze remained fixed on Darcy.

Her head tilted so that her hair fell in a glossy curtain, she looked back at him, mesmerized. *He's talking to me*, Darcy realized, her hands sweating on the steering wheel. *With those eyes and that voice, he's tempting me.*

And she was ready for the temptation. *I don't want to go home this time*, Darcy thought. *I want the real world.*

But she couldn't speak; her tongue was paralyzed. She waited anxiously, eagerly for Caro's response.

"Maybe we are," Caro said, cool and casual.

The guy lit the cigarette, his eyes now on the light which had just gone green. "I'm Nick. See you there."

The Camaro peeled out. The BMW, meanwhile, stalled. Darcy snapped herself back to reality. Or was it reality? The ghost of James Dean had just invited her, Darcy Jenner, to a party out on the town limits. In the badlands. For a millisecond, Darcy wished she really *were* safe at the movies with Sue Rhiner.

"Well, Darce, what d'ya think?" Caro's eyes sparkled a dare in the dark.

Darcy restarted the engine. *You only live once — might as well live wild,* she thought. And after all, she wasn't alone; she had Caro to back her up.

Grinning at Caro, Darcy floored it in pursuit of the Camaro. "Let's check it out."

Easing open the back door, Darcy stepped into the dark kitchen, pocketing her house key. The grandfather clock ticked steadily, the only sound in the sleeping house.

Her heart ricocheting around under her ribs, Darcy skated up the back stairs skipping the creaky ones. Maybe it was stupid to be so cautious — her parents couldn't possibly hear her, their rooms being in the other wing of the house — but Darcy was paranoid. Four in the morning was kind of late for a night at the movies, even a triple feature. They wouldn't buy it.

Safe in her own room, she flopped back on the bed, exhaling a huge sigh of relief. *I made it. Home free.*

Then Darcy shut her eyes and her head started whirling. *I shouldn't have been driving. . . . How many beers did I have?* Nick had probably slipped four or five bottles of Bud into her hand, though she did pour at least half of each out on the dirt when nobody was looking.

Darcy thumped a hand on her chest, telling her heart to slow down. But it didn't, and she had a feeling that even though it was incredibly late she was going to have a hard time falling asleep. She was too keyed up.

Remembered scenes flashed across the moon-dappled bedroom ceiling as Darcy stared up. The dead-end dirt road . . . a circle of beat-up cars . . . somebody's car stereo cranking metal. A dozen kids, among them Nick, his red-brown hair catching light from the crackling bonfire. He'd been expecting them.

The girl in faded jeans and a baggy black sweater, her dark hair loose and tangled. *Was that me?* Darcy wondered, shivering with a sudden chill. She pulled her comforter around her shoulders. *Yes — and no.*

It had been fun. Easy as anything. Like playing charades, acting a part. Darcy had talked and laughed with Nick and his friends as if she were one of them, her BMW not withstanding. And she made an impression. She was the one, not Caro, Nick came on to. It was her phone number that Nick scratched on the inside of a book of matches. She was the one Nick kissed. . . .

The blood rushed into Darcy's face as she remembered, her body trembling again now just as it had then, when Nick's hard, muscular arms were around her. He'd pulled her aside, his hands not rough but not gentle either, out of the dancing circle of light cast by the bonfire. He hadn't said anything — Nick didn't seem to be much of a guy for words. Just gripped her shoulders and put his mouth on hers. The kiss was long — hot — dizzying.

She'd pulled back from Nick's embrace, thrilled and terrified. Nobody had ever kissed her like that —

none of the prep-school boys she'd dated, not even the one she got kicked out of Merton for. And Nick had wanted more. He'd tried to pull her down on the pine needles, but Darcy backed off, saying she wanted another beer, although really she just wanted to assure herself that Caro was still there. She was, of course, and luckily had been too busy talking to a cute guy with a mustache to notice Darcy's smooch with Nick.

Darcy groaned, burying her face in the soft fuzzy body of Waldo the stuffed walrus who lived on her bed. Then she giggled. *I can't believe I was embarrassed that Caro might have seen me kiss Nick when one beer later I was dancing on the hood of somebody's Buick! Talk about making a spectacle of myself.*

She and Caro had left when the party was at its wildest, not having realized it was so late. Darcy had felt like Cinderella in reverse, hurrying home before she turned back into a debutante.

Now she undressed and then crawled under the covers, hugging Waldo with one arm. In the moonlight, Darcy's room was peaceful and comforting. Everything in it was *old*. The colony of dolls and animals on the shelves, the bulletin board with shriveled corsages and torn-out pictures from magazines dating back years. Home. Things here had been more tense than ever since the blow-up after the charge card episode; Darcy still felt like she was on trial with her parents. But no matter what, home was home, the place she could always come back to for security and protection, as solid as a rock.

So why am I scared? Darcy asked herself, snuggling

under the down comforter. Why did her room look the same, but different? Why did she feel the same, but different?

"It's not like I left my glass slipper behind at the party," she pointed out to Waldo. But she had given Nick her number, for all purposes the same thing. She didn't even know his last name.

Suddenly the security of her house, her world, seemed a little shaky.

"So — you're going to hate me — I told my parents I was going to a movie with you." Darcy paused in her story as the butler came into the Rhiners' dining room to fill the orange-juice glasses, then took up a post by the sideboard.

Sue scanned the row of silver serving dishes in a disinterested fashion. "I'll just have eggs and a muffin, Joseph."

Darcy watched as Joseph filled a plate for Sue, resisting the urge to laugh. The weekend brunch routine at the Rhiners' had always seemed slightly ridiculous to her. The sideboard was set up like a serve-yourself buffet, except you didn't serve yourself — Joseph served you. *When it comes to pointless pomposity*, Darcy thought, *the Rhiners outdo even my family*.

"I'd like a waffle. And some of that yogurt and fruit," she said. "Thanks, Joseph."

After placing the plates on the table, Joseph departed and Darcy and Sue had the lofty dining room to themselves.

"You're incredibly lucky, Darce," Sue observed, shaking salt and pepper onto her eggs. "I almost called your house last night to see if you wanted to get together. You would've been nailed."

"Tell me about it." Darcy felt sick just at the thought. "For the record, we saw the new Mel Gibson movie and went for pizza."

"Don't worry, I'll cover for you," Sue promised. "So, what is it you were up to that you had to be so devious?"

Darcy studied her friend over the rim of her juice glass. Sue was going to love this. "Well, I wasn't up to anything at first. Just driving around downtown with Caroline."

Sue's skeptical expression made it clear that she thought this sounded bad enough in itself. "Just driving around?" she repeated.

"You know. Cruising," Darcy said mischievously, knowing full well the word was *not* in Sue Rhiner's vocabulary.

"Cruising." Sue shook her head, mystified. There was another lull in the conversation as Joseph reappeared to pour coffee. "You mean you cruised till four in the morning?"

"Three-thirty. I had to drop Caro off on my way home."

"Okay, three-thirty!" Sue exclaimed, laughing into her coffee. "You cruised till three-thirty in the morning?"

"No. We met this guy. . . ."

Sue was interested. "What guy? Where?"

"This guy Nick somebody. At an intersection. Caro

talked to him. You know, they both had their windows down. And he invited us to this party out on Sand Hill Road."

"You didn't go," Sue said. "Tell me you didn't go to a party with some guy you met at a *stoplight*."

"Sure." Darcy shrugged carelessly, as if she did it all the time. "He was outrageously good-looking. Real tough and cool, with these deep-set James Dean eyes."

"Darcy, I don't believe you," Sue declared. Then she looked puzzled. "Sand Hill? Off Cross County Road? But nobody lives out there. It's just woods."

"Well, the party wasn't at a *house*." Darcy couldn't help enjoying Sue's shock. "It was just a bunch of cars parked around. People and a couple of cases of beer. That's all you need, don't you think?"

"You really want to know what I think?" Sue demanded, buttering her muffin vigorously.

"Give it to me straight," said Darcy, smiling.

Sue didn't smile back. "I think you're an idiot! Picking up some guy on a street corner and then going to some dead-end road in the badlands in the middle of the night. What kind of thing is that to do?"

"You make it sound like I sold my body to Satan," Darcy responded dryly. "I didn't break any laws." She remembered the beer. "Well, not any big ones . . . "

"Darce, I'm not talking about laws. I mean, that wasn't just some prep-school prank. It was stupid. And dangerous."

"I don't happen to see it that way," Darcy said airily. "I had a good time. A really good time. It was just people having fun. Is that so offensive?" Her tone darkened. "I guess maybe it is. It's a sure bet none of them, Nick or the rest, went to prep school or belong to the country club or get breakfast served to them by a goddamn *butler*. Their names aren't in the social register."

"Forget it, if you're going to be so irrational." Darcy saw the hurt in Sue's eyes. "I only said what I said because you're my friend and I care about you. But if you won't see it that way, then let's just drop it, okay?"

"I'm sorry." Now Darcy felt terrible for snapping off Sue's head like that. "Maybe I shouldn't even have told you."

"I just don't understand you," Sue said, pushing her plate away. "I *want* to understand you, Darce, I really do. I just don't get what you're trying to prove."

"I'm not trying to prove anything," Darcy protested, not sure, however, if that was entirely true. "I just want . . . I don't know. To be myself."

"What, and like you *weren't* yourself before you started hanging around with Caroline Buchanan and 'cruising' and all that?" Sue asked, puzzled.

"No. I don't think I was," Darcy confessed.

Sue was quiet for a moment. Then she lifted her shoulders. "Darcy, I just don't know what to say. You know I'll always be on your side, whatever you do. You're my oldest friend. If the subject ever comes up, of course I'll back you up about last night. But in the future . . . " Sue dropped her eyes. "I guess I'd appreciate it if you didn't use my name when you lie to your parents about where you go at night. I just don't feel right about it."

"Don't worry." Darcy sipped her coffee and then put down the china cup; it was cold. She looked at

Sue, feeling a little sad. Even though they were sitting only a couple feet apart, Darcy had never felt so far from her.

Since last night, and Nick, everything's changed, Darcy realized. Things had been changing for her ever since she started going to Norwell but right now, talking to Sue like this, it was clear to Darcy for the first time that there was no going back. Maybe the time had come to make a choice. Sue and Saturday brunch with the butler; her old life, the unreal existence of sixteen sheltered years. Or Caro and T.J. and Josh and Nick . . . and freedom.

Darcy sighed. "Don't worry, Sue," she repeated. "I won't use your name like that again."

From now on I'm on my own.

TWELVE

"What are you doing for dinner tonight?" Darcy asked Caroline as they slipped into adjacent back-row seats in their homeroom.

"You want to go out?" Caro's eyes, cat-green in the morning light, twinkled slyly. "Maybe hunt up Nick?"

Darcy laughed and flushed. "That's *not* what I had in mind," she said. "I just wanted to know, if you didn't have plans, if you wanted to come over to my house for dinner."

Squeak. Mrs. Simison, the homeroom teacher, went at the blackboard with a fresh piece of chalk. Caroline winced. "Your house?" she repeated, clearly surprised.

Darcy expected this reaction. "Yeah, well, I can't promise it'll be *fun* — the place isn't Disneyland. But I want to have you over. You've never been to my house, and besides, my parents really want to meet some of my new friends. I thought I'd see if Alison could come, too."

My parents want to meet some of my new friends — Darcy bit her lip, half regretting her invitation already. It was a gamble. But Darcy was determined. She'd made up her mind the other day after Nick, and Sue. No more hiding her new friends and her new self. She'd spent enough years dancing to somebody else's tune.

The hard part would be telling her mother later that there were going to be unexpected guests for dinner. But it was the only way — she had to spring it on her, go for the element of surprise. Her mom would never agree otherwise; she'd think up a thousand excuses.

They'll change their minds when they meet Caro and Alison and see how nice they are, Darcy tried to convince herself. *Underneath their stuffy class-conscious facades my parents aren't monsters.*

"Sure, I'll come over to the Jenner mansion for dinner," Caro said, teasing. "Is it a formal affair?"

"Black tie, of course," Darcy joked back. "I usually wear my best jeans. I'll drive over, pick you up around six, okay?"

"Not necessary." Caro smiled with pure happiness. "The Mustang's coming home from the shop today. I've got wheels again."

The late bell rang just as a last bunch of kids jostled their way through the homeroom door, T.J. and Josh among them. T.J. threw his books on the desk in front of Caro's, and Darcy caught them stealing a quick hand squeeze.

Slumping into an empty seat, Josh glanced at Darcy. Fast, like he didn't want to but felt he should. Darcy smiled, friendly and hopeful. A flicker of warmth crossed Josh's face, then he gave her his profile, staring forward at the back of Marc Calamano's head.

Darcy sighed, tracing her pen in the graffiti grooves on the desk top. Was Josh ever going to come around?

They were in the sun room that afternoon, Mrs. Jenner reading a Smith College alumnae magazine, Darcy writing up her chemistry lab report. The atmosphere was peaceful and warm. *I hate to ruin it*, Darcy thought, glancing at her mother out of the corner of her eye. The two of them didn't share many quiet moments like this. *Mom never has a problem finding something to pick on me about, and here I go handing her an excuse on a silver platter.*

But maybe it didn't have to be that way. Darcy doodled thoughtfully in the margin of her chem notebook. She'd been fed up lately because her parents didn't give her a chance. Maybe she needed to give *them* a chance — a chance to prove they loved her enough to let her grow.

"Mom, I invited a couple friends over for dinner. I already told Colleen there'd be extra people and she's setting two more places." Darcy rattled the speech off fast, silently congratulating herself on the inspiration of presenting her mother with a *fait accompli*. Then she waited, breath in check, for a response.

Mrs. Jenner looked up with a show of interest. She

closed the magazine, carefully keeping her place with one finger. "Friends for dinner? That's nice, honey. We haven't seen Sue in a while. But you said two people?"

Darcy's eyes narrowed. Her mother knew perfectly well she wasn't talking about Sue. She was just going to make this as difficult as possible. "Not Sue, Caroline Buchanan and Alison Laurel. Girls from Norwell. You don't know them," she said evenly.

To Darcy's surprise her mother didn't object. Instead she smiled. "Well, I guess that will change as of this evening, hmm? I'll look forward to meeting them." She flipped open her magazine and resumed reading.

Darcy stared at her, not sure whether to feel triumphant or suspicious. She wished she could read her mother's mind. But Mrs. Jenner was impenetrably serene and self-contained. The late-afternoon sun sparkled on her blond-frosted hair, glinted off her raw-silk trousers and tunic. Glossy magazine pages turned with leisurely regularity. She wasn't giving anything away.

Darcy didn't know what to think. It had been too easy. Since the day she had started public high school, her mother hadn't had one nice thing to say about any of the kids from Norwell. Or about her, for that matter. There had to be a catch.

At six o'clock Darcy started watching out the west parlor window. As she stood gazing idly at the streaks of sunset color in the autumn sky, she fell to daydreaming about Nick. It was a few days now since the party . . . and she still couldn't shake the memory of what it felt like to be in his arms. Was he going to call her or not? At the thought that she might never see him again, Darcy felt a sharp pang of disappointment. No, she decided. He had to call. He had to want to kiss her again like he did that night at the party. *She* wanted to kiss him again, that was for sure.

Darcy half closed her eyes, fantasizing. He'd call — his voice urgent with pent-up desire. They'd go out . . . where? *What's a guy like Nick's idea of a date, anyhow?* she wondered. Whatever it was, they'd have to meet someplace — which was much sexier anyway than having him pick her up at her house. She could never in a million years introduce him to her parents. . . .

At twenty minutes past, Caroline's steel blue '65 Mustang coasted into view, looking pretty good considering it'd been driven into a brick wall not too long ago.

Darcy met Caro and Alison at the front door. "You guys are really nice to come over."

"You're nice to invite us," Alison responded, smiling as she darted a curious look around.

"Yeah, really." Caro shrugged out of her leather jacket. "Where should I put this, Darce?"

"Oh, I'll take it." Darcy hung Caroline's jacket and Alison's vintage forties overcoat, from the Salvation Army no doubt, in the hall coat closet, suppressing a giggle. Her mother's furs never had such blue-collar company.

Then she turned back to her friends. They made a striking contrast with the elegantly decorated front hall — and with one another. Alison, looking a little bit nervous, was dressed almost formally in a brocade-print skirt, lacy blouse, and fringed scarf. Caro, meanwhile, had taken Darcy at her word and worn her best jeans and a man's suit vest over a pink T-shirt.

"We eat around seven but my parents usually have a drink before dinner," Darcy explained, leading the way into the parlor. "They'll drift in any minute. What do you guys want?"

"Vodka martini, shaken not stirred," Caro joked.

"Can I see I.D., miss?" Darcy rejoined. "You do have a choice, though. Club soda or diet soda or soda soda."

Glasses in hand, the three girls sat for a moment just sipping. The parlor appeared enormous and museumlike, even to Darcy. The same room that had been just right for the D.A.R. tea suddenly seemed ridiculous occupied by three teenaged girls.

Alison broke the somewhat awkward silence. "This is a beautiful room, Darcy," she said sincerely. "I've never seen a prettier Persian rug. I love it. See, Caro? All the little people and animals woven among the leafy pattern. It's like a tapestry, it tells a story."

Caroline obediently admired the carpet. Then she peered at Darcy. "Do we get to snoop around the rest of the house?"

"I thought maybe after dinner." Darcy hadn't wanted to urge a grand tour and seem as if she were showing off. "Right now I'd really like for you to meet my parents. They should be making an appearance any minute."

But Mr. and Mrs. Jenner didn't show. Caro and Alison, gossiping about Marc, didn't seem to sense anything amiss, but Darcy became more and more tense as time passed. No doubt about it, it was an intentional gesture. Her parents were probably having cocktails in the library, deliberately avoiding her guests. *Are they going to boycott dinner, too?* Darcy wondered anxiously. *Announce they're eating out?* How would she explain *that* to her friends?

It didn't happen that way, however. At seven, Darcy ushered Caroline and Alison into the dining room where five places were set. A moment later, her mother entered, exuding about as much warmth as a glacier, Darcy thought. Her father followed, carrying two bottles of wine which he handed to Colleen with instructions to set them chilling. *Icy, everything's going to be icy*, Darcy thought with sudden uncomfortable foresight.

"Mom and Dad, this is Alison Laurel, and this is Caroline Buchanan," she announced cheerfully.

Her father shook hands, his manner disinterested but friendly. "Hello, girls. Welcome."

Mrs. Jenner extended her hand as well, smiling as graciously as if she were greeting the royal family. "I'm happy to meet the new friends Darcy's been telling me so much about," she said. Alison smiled widely, eager to please. Caro's lips curved slightly, her eyes grey and cautious. "And I hope this will be the first of many visits," Mrs. Jenner added. "Let's sit down, shall we?"

Darcy sat down but she didn't relax. If she didn't know her mother, she'd think Mrs. Jenner was being sweet and hospitable. But she knew her mother.

Colleen came in to serve soup and distribute salad

plates. Darcy saw Alison and Caro exchange glances. She'd never thought much about having servants; now Darcy felt self-conscious. She barely acknowledged Colleen as Colleen slid a salad plate next to her elbow.

There was a brief pause before anyone began eating. Mrs. Jenner watched discreetly as Alison hesitated with her hand suspended over the array of silverware next to her plate. Darcy chose a spoon and Alison, following her example, did the same.

"So, Alison." Mrs. Jenner began the conversation, sounding sincerely interested. "Now that you've met Darcy's family, tell us about your own. What does your father do?"

Darcy nearly choked on a piece of crab from the bisque. Across the table Caroline stiffened, but Alison remained composed, although two tiny spots of pink colored her cheeks. "My father . . . is no longer part of my family," she said softly but with dignity.

"Does your mother work?" Mrs. Jenner asked, her eyes fixed on Alison who was now studying the fork selection. Darcy touched her own salad fork, hoping Alison would catch the cue.

"Yes, ma'am," Alison confirmed, to Darcy's relief spearing a cherry tomato with the correct fork. "She's a housekeeper."

Darcy waited in dread. What was her mother going to say next? Offer Mouse congratulations that her mom had managed to stay off welfare?

Mrs. Jenner just smiled. "How nice," she observed with emphasis, as if the housekeeping profession were one she herself had always aspired to.

Darcy looked apologetically at Alison who gave her a small it's-all-right smile.

Colleen appeared silently to whisk away the soup and salad plates, and Darcy sat up with a start. Alison's mother was a housekeeper — and so was Colleen. Somehow, this realization put Colleen in a different perspective. *All these years I've treated Colleen the way my parents do — as if the sole reason she exists is to serve us. How can she stand it — or us?*

Mr. Jenner's voice broke into Darcy's thoughts. "Excuse me for not offering you girls some wine, but as Darcy can testify, she's only allowed to partake on holidays."

"Right." Darcy picked up on his remark, glad for an opportunity to redirect her thoughts. "At church my folks won't even let me take wine from the Communion tray," she explained with a teasing smile for her father. "I have to drink grape juice like the preschoolers."

Darcy caught Caro's eye on the wine bottle as Mr. Jenner liberally refilled his glass. Half gone and they were still on the first course. *Great, he's picked tonight to drink like a fish.* He'd been doing that a lot lately, she realized.

Darcy was growing more uncomfortable by the second, but she was determined not to give up. So her mother had pried out the appalling truth that Alison came from a working-class single-parent family. Now it was time she learned how interesting and talented Alison was. "Mom, Alison's involved with theater arts at school, and she sings in a band. She's excellent. Isn't she, Caro?"

Caroline nodded, her eyes glinting warily in the muted light of the chandelier.

Mrs. Jenner dabbed at her mouth with a linen napkin. "I might have guessed that," she said with a glance at Alison's Gypsy-look outfit. "And what about you, Caroline? Are you interested in theater as well?"

Caroline tipped her head, cool under Mrs. Jenner's sweet, sharp scrutiny. "No, theater's not my line. I'm too busy."

"What *are* your interests, dear?" Mrs. Jenner pursued.

Darcy froze, her hands clenching the linen napkin in her lap. What if Caro came right out with the truth? Said that she went cruising in her Mustang, stayed out all night, slept around, and skipped school occasionally?

But Caroline responded to the question in good faith, just as if it had been asked in the same. "I like tennis and listening to music. I drive places — try to see the world, you know?"

Mrs. Jenner nodded and to Darcy's intense relief apparently decided to let the matter of Caro's "interests" rest there. *I don't know how much more of this my nerves can stand*, Darcy thought.

The door to the dining room opened, and Colleen reappeared with the main course. Darcy felt a guilty twinge at her appearance. This time, though, she said thanks as the housekeeper served her. Colleen lifted one brow in surprise, then went on to set down Caroline's and Alison's dishes.

As the group picked at the entree, Darcy's father came to the conversational rescue, sort of. The first bottle of wine was empty and the second uncorked. Darcy listened, mortified, as he started in on a Life-styles-of-the-Rich-and-Famous-type anecdote, dropping names and net worths left and right. The two guests just chewed wordlessly, Alison nodding frequently while Caro looked bland and removed. Darcy tried to switch her father onto another track, but to no avail. He just started cheerfully in on another glass of wine and another long-winded story.

Over coffee and cake, Mrs. Jenner turned again to Caroline. Darcy felt vaguely ill as her mother popped the expected innocently insinuating question about Caro's family. *Why couldn't the meal have ended before we got to this point?*

"My family?" Caro said, leaning her elbows on the table with a tight, polite smile that didn't reach her eyes. "My family's kind of small. My mom ran out on us a long time ago, so it's just me and Dad."

Mrs. Jenner was ready to make another remark, but Darcy didn't dare risk it. A little more of this and Caro might be pushed too far. Dropping her napkin on the table, Darcy pushed back her chair. "Dad, can we be excused? I want to show Alison and Caroline my bedroom."

As soon as the three were out of the dining room, Caro made a beeline for the coat closet, Alison trailing. Darcy hurried after them. "Do you want to hang around for a while?" she asked. "We could go up to my room and listen to music or something —"

"I just remembered I have to be some place," Caro said flatly, pulling her jacket off the hanger.

Trying to lighten the scene, Alison started to remove a fur coat from the closet. "Oops! I forgot, I didn't wear my mink!" she kidded.

Darcy's mouth smiled but her eyes sparkled with tears. Meanwhile Caroline was already at the door. Darcy and Alison followed her out to the driveway.

"Caro, Alison. I'm sorry." Darcy folded her arms across her chest, shivering as the cold night air whipped around her. "I know my dad's a preppy bore and my mom was really nosey. I'm sorry dinner turned out to be a drag. I didn't want it to happen that way."

Alison put a hand on Darcy's arm. "It's okay, Darcy. We understand. And anyhow, dinner was fabulous. I'll eat Colleen's cooking any day."

Darcy turned to Caro, needing assurance that she understood, too. The wind blew the long, shimmering hair back from Caro's face. Her expression was unreadable. "I've got to be some place," she repeated, avoiding Darcy's gaze.

"Please don't be mad at me, Caro," Darcy begged. "I didn't plan this. I just wanted my parents to meet my new friends. I wanted them to like you guys as much as I do." Brushing a tear from the side of her nose, she stammered to a stop.

Caroline's expression softened. "It's okay, Darce," she said gruffly. "The whole scene just put me on edge. I know it wasn't your fault." She smiled ironically as she slid into the driver's seat. "Like Mouse said, it was a four-star meal. Better than heating up a Stouffer's or ordering Chinese."

Inside the car, Alison rolled down the passenger-side window a few inches. "See you in school tomorrow, okay?" she called, her breath clouding in the frosty air.

Darcy waved as Caro gave the Mustang some gas. She watched the headlights bob up the driveway and turn onto High Ridge, then fade into the dark and disappear.

It didn't work, she thought sadly, standing alone in the wind. She'd brought her two worlds together and they didn't mix.

"I feel sorry for her," Alison confessed as they hit a wide open stretch on High Ridge and Caroline floored it.

"You mean, like poor little rich girl, that sort of thing?"

Alison heard the bitter note in her friend's usually mellow voice. "C'mon, Caro," she said gently. "Dinner was as hard on her as it was on us. I think she really felt terrible."

"You're right," Caroline conceded at last. "I just could've done without meeting Lord and Lady Jenner. Nobody's ego needs a kick in the face like that, you know? To sit there and have somebody let you know they don't think you're good enough to hang out with their kid . . ."

Alison sighed into the turned-up collar of her overcoat. "Everybody's got something to fight against. Now we know about Darcy."

"Ain't that the truth!"

Alison's street was quietly warm with lights from

the rows of apartment buildings. Caroline rolled to a stop by the Laurels' building.

"What are you going to do?" asked Alison before getting out of the car.

Caro shrugged, patting the steering wheel with a throaty chuckle. "Drive all night maybe. I've missed this baby. Or go over to T.J.'s. One or the other."

"Have fun. And thanks for the ride. See ya, sweet-ie!"

" 'Night, Mouse."

The Mustang rumbled off. Alison paused for a moment as she opened the door to the front hall, drinking in the sharp, clean air and the music of the night — wind piping through the bare tree branches, the rustling conversation of dry leaves.

Inside, though, there wasn't any music, just the T.V. Some game show, where you could watch Joe Ordinary win mountains of cash. The American dream. Alison followed the tube's blare to the living room where her mom, who'd obviously just gotten home from work, was sacked out on the couch, shoes kicked off and feet elevated. There was a run in her mother's stocking and for some stupid reason it made Alison want to cry. It completed the picture and made it almost too tired and sad to bear.

"Ma, you look beat," Alison observed, perching on the scuffed La-Z-Boy.

"Honey, hi." Mrs. Laurel lifted her head. Her young, worn face brightened with a fond smile. "I *am* beat. Where'd you come from?"

"Oh, I had dinner over at a friend's house," Alison explained.

Her mother dropped her head again. "That's good. I just got in half an hour ago. Had to work late and Benjie and Woofer still haven't had supper. They must've gotten fed up waiting — they're nowhere to be found."

"I'll put something together for them," Alison offered. "They'll turn up when they smell Spaghetti-O's!"

Her mom's dry crinkly laugh reminded Alison of the autumn leaves outside. *There is music in this house,* she thought. *You just have to listen for it.*

Hopping to her feet, Alison moved to the sofa, squeezing next to her mother and giving her a quick kiss. She gazed, concerned, into the soft, shadowed brown eyes so much like her own. "What about you? Can I fix something for you?"

"No thanks, honey bear. I had a sandwich at the Andersons'."

"I'll make us a cup of tea then," Alison said, patting her mother's hand.

The kitchen was dingy and cluttered, breakfast dishes still piled in the sink, the table scattered with newspapers and unopened mail. Alison and her mom split the housework, but even so they never seemed to get it all done. Alison imagined Darcy's family, with a cook and a maid. Then she pushed the picture from her mind.

With one hand Alison ran soapy water into the sink, switching the gas on under the kettle with the other. She didn't like to think about it but sometimes, like now, it was impossible not to. Her mom — thirty-five, a single parent, holding down a job she didn't

like. Probably working as somebody else's drudge for
the rest of her life.

And lonely. Mom and me both, Alison recognized.
Even with the band, theater stuff at school, her mom
and Benjie and Woofer, the house to take care of; even
with Caro and Darcy. *I'm lonely.*

The house was small, the kitchen cramped, but
right then it felt as enormous and empty and echoing
as the Jenners'. There was room for something . . .
someone . . .

The tea kettle whistled shrilly and Alison thought
about Marc.

THIRTEEN

Darcy turned to face the house, sure of herself and of what she was going to say. *No hysterical bawling*, she coached herself. *No yelling. I'm just going to tell them straight what I think. Who I am and how I want to live.*

Her parents were still in the dining room, lingering over coffee. Both glanced up quickly as Darcy entered, as if they were ready for an outburst.

Looking at them, Darcy experienced a puzzled, angry, aching sensation. It was weird to feel something like hate toward the people she loved most in the world.

"I can't believe the way you treated my friends," she began, her tone steady. "I was ashamed of you, and ashamed of myself for being your daughter."

"Darcy, sweetheart." Her father smoothed the air

with his hands, as if it were Darcy's ruffled feathers. "I think you're overreacting."

"Like hell I'm overreacting!" Darcy shouted despite her resolution to stay calm.

"Darcy, there's no need to raise your voice," Mrs. Jenner said, her own voice cool and unaffected. "And there's no need, nor do you have the right, to criticize your father and me."

"I think I do have the right," Darcy declared. "This is my life we're talking about, and I'm not going to let you dictate to me any longer."

"We don't dictate to you, honey." Mrs. Jenner tried a softer tone. "Caroline and Alison came over for dinner, didn't they?"

"Yes, and you made damn sure they'd never want to set foot in this house again!" Darcy swallowed a throatful of frustrated, disappointed tears. "That's what you wanted, Mom, wasn't it?" she whispered. "You think if you stay on my case and stay on my case and stay on my case, some day I'll turn into Sarah and you can get crowned D.A.R. Mother of the Decade. Well, it's not going to happen."

To Darcy's astonishment, her mother's eyes suddenly filled with tears. "None of this would have happened if you hadn't gone to Norwell," Mrs. Jenner said, her voice clipped with suppressed emotion.

"But you sent me there," Darcy pointed out, wishing her mother wouldn't cry. It made it a lot harder to be mad at her. "You thought it would teach me a lesson and it did, but not the one — "

"Do you think we *wanted* you to go to public school?" Mrs. Jenner burst out. Mr. Jenner put a hand on her arm but she ignored him. "Do you think we would have stooped to that instead of finding you another private school if it weren't for the money?"

"Money?" Darcy repeated in confusion, looking from her mother to her father.

Mrs. Jenner drew a deep, uneven breath and leaned back in her chair, smoothing her hand over her hair. Mr. Jenner stirred his coffee, his jaw set in a tense line.

"Would someone tell me what's going on?" Darcy begged. "Dad?"

He met her eyes and sighed in a tired fashion. "Money problems, Darcy," he said at last, without much emotion. "We've been having them for a while."

Darcy digested this, shock rendering her momentarily speechless. Money was the last thing she would ever think any Jenner would have to worry about. Since the time the family fortune was made in the steel industry, it had always been solid. But now, like puzzle pieces, a melange of scattered impressions fell into place. The reference to failed investments the day Grandpa Jenner gave her the car, and the tension between her father and grandfather on numerous other occasions. The country club, her charge card that night at Giapetto's . . . clues left and right and she hadn't even seen them.

"You mean," Darcy said slowly and in disbelief, "the only reason you sent me to Norwell was to save money?"

Her parents nodded and for a brief moment Darcy

almost felt sorry for them. But then the hurt and outrage rushed back in. "You let me think it was punishment — you let me feel like you thought I was a disgrace."

"We were trying to protect you," Mr. Jenner explained.

"And look where it got me," Darcy cried, her eyes smarting with painful tears. "You didn't do me any favors by hiding the truth from me; you were just thinking about yourselves. You care more about your stupid old pride than you do about your own daughter!"

Darcy's hands were pushed deep in the pockets of her jeans, her left fingers clenched tightly around her car keys. Now she yanked the keys out with a jingle.

"Darcy, of course we care about you," her father protested.

"And money is not really the issue here," said Mrs. Jenner, her eyes dry once more. "We're still your parents, and as such, you're our responsibility. I think we've all had enough shouting. Honey, hand me the keys. You're not going out tonight." She stuck out her hand.

Darcy pocketed the keys. "I'll do what I want, Mother."

"Hand me the keys," Mrs. Jenner repeated, exasperated.

Darcy shook her head. "I'm not going to obey you, so why don't you kick me out of the house?" she dared them. "Go ahead, Mom, kick me out. Oh, that's right, I forgot — you want it the other way around. You want to keep me here, locked in."

"Don't push me, Darcy," Mrs. Jenner warned.

"I won't push you," she promised, spinning on her boot heel. "I'll save you the trouble. I'm kicking myself out!"

Then she was running, her footsteps echoing in the hall, drowning out the sound of her father's voice calling her back.

Her car, her ally, was waiting in the garage. Darcy hit the switch on the wall, sending the automatic garage door rolling upward.

Jump behind the wheel, key in the ignition; shift into reverse and give it gas; back up, tires screeching; haul on the wheel and point down the driveway. Go.

Slicing through the night in the BMW, Darcy felt like a space capsule jettisoned from the mother ship. She was floating through space, totally detached and free. *Maybe I'll never go back,* she thought seriously. What was there to go back to? Parents who hid their real troubles and then made it look as if she was the problem; parents who would never be able to accept her as a person in her own right.

If the whole thing weren't such a nightmare, Darcy almost could have laughed. Money, of all things. So there wasn't as much of it as there used to be, which meant, when all was said and done, she really *was* on a level with her new friends from Nowhere High.

Turning on the radio, Darcy remembered something. Caro had her car back which meant that maybe she was still on the road, cruising, in which case Darcy could catch up with her and apologize again for the scene at dinner, really talk things over.

Darcy headed downtown. On a weeknight like this Redmond was a ghost town, until you reached the strip.

She turned up the volume on the radio, taking comfort in the loud pulse of rock. *I'm on the strip, cruising,* she realized. *Without Caro, by myself.* It was more exciting and a lot scarier. Darcy's heart rate easily outstripped the beat of the heavy-metal song on the radio.

There were lots of cars, but no familiar Mustang convertible. Darcy circled around the block onto Seventh Street, running out of steam. "You kicked yourself out of the house," she reminded herself boldly. "You're not going home tonight."

Then Darcy knew where she could go. There was one person who was always easy to find on a weeknight. It wasn't eleven yet — Josh was sure to be at Jake's Place.

So what am I going to say to him? Darcy wondered. For a few minutes, she wracked her brain. Then she knew. This time, she couldn't just deliver a prepared speech the way she did when she'd apologized to him at T.J.'s birthday party. This time, she wanted to talk *with* Josh, back and forth, give and take. This time, for the first time, she felt that she could really do that.

The next intersection was Coville. Darcy hung a left, her eye on Jake's parking lot. A drawn-out, vibrating guitar lick killed the song on the radio just as Darcy's heart called a time out.

In the burger stand parking lot, the neon lights sparking off its long, low hood, was Nick's Camaro.

Darcy gulped, letting up on the gas. Her brain and the BMW both rolled along in slow motion. *Keep on driving,* her old cowardly instincts told her. *Don't stop if you know what's good for you.*

"If it was Caro, what would she do?" Darcy asked out loud. She bit her lip, feeling as if she were split right down the middle.

There was an empty parking space next to Nick's car. Instead of continuing straight on the road, Darcy turned into the lot, knowing she was really crossing a line this time. And there'd be no going back.

Darcy got out and walked around the back of the BMW toward Nick's car. Nick had rolled down his window. Darcy bent at the waist, resting her crossed arms on the door of the Camaro. Inside it smelled like smoke, greasy burgers, and beer.

"Remember me?" Darcy asked, sounding a lot bolder than she felt.

"Remember you? You're kidding." Nick looked over his shoulder at his two buddies. They grinned, checking Darcy out like she was a magazine centerfold. Turning back to her, Nick smiled, slow and meaningful. "Ask these clowns. I was just tellin' them about this very hot, mysterious little girl I met the other night who I've been thinkin' about calling."

Nick's face was very near hers. The lawless expression in his eyes gave Darcy goose bumps. "Well, you don't have to call," she said flirtatiously. "Here I am."

"Here you are. That's right." Nick glanced again at the other guys. "You gentlemen don't mind if I ditch you for a while, eh? Gonna buy the lady a drink."

The guys laughed, as if Nick were talking in code and they got something out of his words she didn't. Darcy's spine tingled.

"Hey, and take care of my wheels," Nick warned his friends. "One scratch and you're dead meat, both of ya."

The Camaro door slammed and Nick was standing on the pavement, looking down at her with those sexy, brooding James Dean eyes. He was taller than Darcy remembered, and older, probably about twenty-five, she figured. She had a sudden urge to run inside the burger stand and hide behind the take-out counter. It wasn't too late to look for Josh. . . .

But she couldn't resist the chance to be with Nick. "I don't feel like a drink," Darcy said cautiously.

"Me either." Nick put a hand on each of her shoulders. His hands were heavy. "How 'bout a spin in your pretty automobile?"

"Sure," Darcy agreed, liking the element of safety in the idea. They'd be on the move and she'd be in the driver's seat.

"Where'd a young girl like you get the money for wheels like this, anyway?" Now Nick's hands were on the BMW, feeling the hard gloss of the paint.

Darcy bit her lip. The last thing she wanted Nick to think about her was that she was a spoiled rich kid. "Oh, I deal a little at school," she said glibly, not expecting him to take her seriously.

Nick raised his thick eyebrows. "That a fact."

"Sure," Darcy answered, playing it cool.

Then she tensed, startled. Nick was easing a hand into the front pocket of her jeans. Smiling, he produced the car keys. "Mind if I drive, babe?"

"Oh!" Darcy stepped away from him, her back against the car. "No, go ahead. You drive."

Somewhat reluctantly, she slid into the passenger seat and fastened her seatbelt. But then as Nick put the BMW through its paces for a few blocks on Coville she relaxed. He was a good driver, and he looked good driving — more like a fantasy come to life than ever. Darcy pressed the automatic window button and shook her head as the wind ripped through her hair. *This is it*, she thought, swept up by the same wild, free rush she'd experienced the night she met Nick. She turned glittering eyes to him, and he smiled knowingly in response, putting his hand on her knee. Sure, she was a little bit scared, just like she'd been then, but that was what made it exciting.

At the Route 58 intersection, Nick pointed the car north. He was heading out of town.

"So, Nick." Darcy lifted her voice above the roar of the engine and the wind. "What do you do, during the day? I mean, for a job?"

Nick lifted his hand from her knee long enough to shift gears. Then the hand was back, on her thigh this time. "I work," he answered.

"Oh." Darcy brushed the hair from her face. "Where?"

"The mill."

Darcy nodded, trying not to freeze up as Nick shifted into fifth on the wide-open highway. The speedometer crested ninety and continued to climb.

She waited for him to ask *her* a question or two. When he didn't Darcy made another attempt at a conversation. "Where do you live?"

"Around here," Nick said, glancing at her in a way that implied he thought she was wasting her breath making small talk.

He sure doesn't talk much, Darcy thought, watching Nick's profile. *A man of deeds, not words?* The nervous feeling in her stomach blossomed into something like fear. "Where are we going, anyway?" she asked, hoping she didn't sound desperate.

Nick didn't even look at her. "Some place you'll like. I promise you," he said, his lips curving.

Darcy stared out the window at the black night, her position becoming breathtakingly clear. *I've got absolutely no control over this situation,* she realized. *No control over Nick, the car, anything.*

God, what an idiot. A guy I hardly know and I let him drive my car with me in it!

Nick had apparently reached comfortable cruising speed. Now he slid a powerful arm around Darcy's shoulders, pulling her closer. Darcy had never felt so helpless in her entire life.

"So, Darcy. Tell me why I haven't seen you around town before. I've usually got my eyes open. I'd've noticed a girl like you, for sure."

For a second she thought maybe she should tell the truth about herself. Tell Nick she was from a rich well-known family. Everybody had heard of the Jenners. Maybe intimidate him a little, regain the upper hand.

The words wouldn't come out. "I-I'm new around here," she stammered, a half-truth anyhow.

"Then I'm glad I found you first before some other guy did," Nick said, flashing her an appreciative look.

"Me, too," Darcy said, not at all glad.

They were heading toward the badlands. The headlights silvered across a familiar sign — Split River Bridge. Darcy gazed at it longingly. Another mile and Nick cut over to Cross County Road. Then he pulled the car off the highway. Sand Hill — the site of the wild party last Friday.

Darcy hoped desperately. *Please let there be dozens of cars at the dead end, another party. Please don't let us be the only ones.*

The street ended in darkness and solitude. No party, no cars; no houses, no nothing. Nick parked, switching the headlights off and killing the engine but leaving the radio on.

First he reclined his seat, and then he pulled a crumpled pack of Camels from the top pocket of his jacket. Darcy watched his every move, fearful and fascinated. As he lit the cigarette, slow and sure of himself, she recovered some of her cool. *Maybe it's going to be okay. He'll have a smoke, we'll talk. I can handle this.*

Nick sucked down some smoke. Then shifting in his seat, he looked at Darcy in a way no guy had ever looked at her. Like he owned her. Like he didn't even have to ask.

"You're so pretty, you know that?" He laughed

huskily through the smoke. "Yeah, you know that. You act like you know you're pretty."

Heat rose into Darcy's face at Nick's words. As scared as she was, she couldn't deny to herself the pleasure she felt because he thought she was pretty. She'd dreamed about him saying things like this to her, and about what would happen next.

Nick inhaled again, the cigarette dissolving into ash. "I wanted to see you again, after the other night," he continued, stubbing the cigarette out against the dashboard.

Darcy nodded. "Me, too," she whispered, her whole body tense, ready for his touch.

Carefully, Nick released Darcy's seatbelt and pushed it aside. For a moment, he paused, his eyes lingering on her face. Darcy held her breath, her heart racing the way the car had been a minute ago. Then Nick's muscular arms went around her and his mouth came down on hers, hard. He was kissing her.

Closing her eyes, Darcy kissed him back, eagerly at first. It was just like the other night; Nick's mouth tasted like smoke, the same way it had then.

Nick's hands moved over Darcy's body, slowly but with purpose and assurance. Her hips, her waist, her shoulders; her flimsy sweater was half off. Darcy's eyes flew open in startled dismay. Wriggling slightly, she tried to work her sweater back down with her elbows, but it was no use. Nick was kissing her with an intensity verging on violence, and she knew he wasn't going to stop there.

What am I going to do? she thought, fighting back

the panic. *Why did I come out here with him?* This wasn't the Nick of her naive fantasies — it was a terrifying stranger. How was she going to get him off her, and get out of there? After the way she'd led him on, Darcy had a fateful feeling Nick wouldn't buy a simple "No."

God, we're so far from town. Darcy squeezed her eyes shut again, inhaling with a low gasp as Nick took his mouth from hers and started to kiss her throat. *No one will hear me if I scream. We're in the goddamn middle of nowhere. . . .*

Then Darcy remembered what else was in the goddamn middle of nowhere and was ready to cry with relief. Split River Station!

She planted both hands on Nick's broad chest and shoved him away abruptly. A dart of anger shot out at her from his black eyes. *Go easy*, she told herself. *Don't get him mad.*

"What's the problem, babe?" There was a warning in his voice, as if he were saying there'd better not *be* any problem.

"No problem," Darcy promised, her breath coming fast. "I just thought of something. A place I know about, where we'd be more comfortable. A deserted place, but with some furniture — a couch."

Nick placed a hand under Darcy's chin, his fingers rough on her skin. "I get your point. Cars ain't ideal when it comes to fooling around. You show me the way and we'll check it out."

As she directed Nick to Split River Station, Darcy prayed silently: *Please somebody be there*. Though she wasn't sure what she could expect if they were.

Darcy knew that some of the gang had a hard time trusting her, maybe even liking her. Caro'd been mad as hell after dinner tonight, and as for Josh . . .

But right now only one thing mattered, only one thing was for certain. At that moment, Darcy needed a friend more than she ever had in her life.

I need you guys. Please somebody be there. . . .

FOURTEEN

At night, in the dark, it felt like it did before they fixed up the station. You could forget the odd pieces of shabby furniture, the dartboard, the Jenners' brass candlesticks. Be alone with the dust and the ghosts of old railway riders, and your own thoughts.

Sprawled out on the sofa, beat from five hot hours behind the grill at Jake's, Josh stared into the moon-speckled gloom. It was cold and his nose was numbing up. He should probably be heading out and home.

A few more minutes . . . Give Dad and the Witch and the brats time to hit the sack. He didn't want to have to deal with any of them, for a change.

The reflection off one of the candlesticks caught his eye. Josh kicked his sneaker against the sofa arm, wishing it was his own head. *Hickham, you're a jerk,* he told himself.

He thought of Darcy, at T.J.'s surprise party, and every day in homeroom. In the cafeteria. Always shooting him one of those dimply, let's-make-up smiles. And he was still hiding behind his hurt pride.

At that Italian restaurant when he had his nervous breakdown, he'd yelled something at Darcy about not being good enough for her. Well, Josh decided now, maybe he really wasn't. Only it wasn't Darcy's attitude that was getting in the way, it was his, his stupid pride. It didn't have anything to do with money, who had it and who didn't. It just had to do with being a fair person, a friend.

I don't have the guts to be Darcy's friend, he realized dismally. Then there was the job at the art supplies store. . . . Somebody else had probably been hired by now. It would serve him right. Life wasn't like that — you couldn't wait around for people and things to fall in your lap.

His eyes still wide open, Josh painted pictures on the black canvas of the air. Faces: Alison's, Darcy's, his dad at dinner listening to the Witch bitch with apathetic whatever-you-say-dear eyes. Faces. *Voices.*

Voices, outside the station. Josh sat up, his heart screeching to a halt like an emergency-braked train. His first quick-flash thought: *Shet Vickers is back in town, here with his gang to finish me off.* Whoever it was knew about the door, though. There were no voices now, just footsteps and the groaning of aged hinges. Two dark forms entered, one big and one small. The big one lit a match and in the yellow circle of light Josh found himself staring at a strange guy — and Darcy.

They saw him at the same instant. Darcy screamed and the guy, equally startled, jumped a couple feet in the air, dropping the match.

Scratch. Another match flamed up with a dry sizzle. "What the . . . ?" the guy exclaimed, looking none too pleased.

It only took a second. Josh's eyes were locked on Darcy's, and it was all there for him to read, as plain as the *Superman* comics on the wall behind him. She was in trouble, in case Josh couldn't have told that from just looking at the guy she was with, who was a hood if he ever saw one. Darcy was in trouble and she needed his help. Her eyes pleaded — and trusted. Trusted *him*. Trusted him to help her figure a way out of whatever mess she'd gotten herself into.

For the first time since he'd known her, Josh felt a genuine bond with Darcy. They were on the same side. They were equals. With his eyes, Josh reached out a hand to Darcy to pull her in.

Wish I knew aikido or karate, or whatever it is T.J. does, he thought nervously. *Could I bluff the guy into believing I'm a black belt? Get your paws off her or I'll smash your face? Dubious.*

"What're you doing here?" Darcy squeaked.

That's my cue. Josh jumped up from the couch. He patted the cushions back into place and then patted his jacket pockets meaningfully. "Clearin' out the stuff. The cops know about this place. They'll be bustin' it wide open any minute."

It took Darcy only a second to get his meaning and run with it. "I told you not to bring it here," she said, sounding furious. "Never mind," she went on quickly. "That last drop-off. How many grams again?"

Josh noted that the guy had also picked up the gist of the conversation and was looking distinctly nervous. *Dude's probably got a record.*

"Forget how much." Josh almost laughed. *I sound like one of the Untouchables!* "A lot. I said the cops'll be showin' up any minute and I meant it. You got your car?"

Darcy nodded. Josh jerked a thumb toward the door. Darcy's "date" was already backing out. "Let's split!"

His Camaro was still there and Nick wanted out the minute they reached the parking lot at Jake's. He kept his cool and a cigarette lit, but he didn't ask Darcy to stick around, which was okay by her.

Darcy only made it three blocks from Jake's after dumping Nick before she had to pull over to the curb and have a thorough collapse. She was laughing hysterically from relief and crying at the same time.

"Guess he didn't want the Feds thinking he was a member of our big-time drug ring." Darcy hugged the steering wheel, her sides aching. "Josh, I swear, you read my mind." She recalled her offhand remark to Nick earlier about how she'd paid for the BMW. "You were too funny."

Josh looked pleased with himself. "I was, wasn't I?"

"I was never so glad to see anybody in my life," Darcy confessed, smudging at the tears with her sweater sleeve. "Honest."

"I'm glad I was there," he said, as if he meant it.

Darcy smiled, the realest smile she'd felt on her face in a long time. Everything had happened so fast that she and Josh had forgotten to be awkward with each other. In the clutch, their misunderstanding about the money at Giapetto's just didn't matter.

"Who was that dude, anyway?" Josh asked.

Darcy laughed wryly. "I don't even really know. Nick somebody. Nick somebody-I-hope-I-never-see-again!"

Josh waited and soon Darcy found herself telling him the whole story. "I met him one night with Caro. We were just driving around, you know? Caro's favorite thing to do. It was fun." Darcy thought back, remembering — the car, the strip, the wild party with Nick, the way it all made her feel so different and so free. "I was trying to be a new person, I guess. Tired of being Darcy Jenner."

"Why?" Turning sideways in the seat, Josh leaned back against the door, his eyes never leaving her. His gaze was steady, curious, kind.

"Why. That's a good question." Darcy took a deep breath. "I don't know, it goes back a long way. Practically all my life. For so many years, I just . . . lived. I mean, I didn't think about who I was, you know? I went to private school, belonged to the country club, was spoiled rotten, and all that. I was a Jenner."

Darcy's English butler drawl made Josh laugh. "And we all know what that means," he kidded.

"Well, yeah. That's my point," Darcy said earnestly. "You think you do, and I used to think I did. But then I got old enough to realize that I didn't really like a lot of the things being a Jenner supposedly was all about. I didn't want to grow up to be just like my mother. Like, I saw where I was going, you know? And it didn't seem like anywhere very interesting."

Darcy stopped, blushing. *What am I doing, boring Josh with my whole life story?*

But he didn't seem bored. "So you signed on at Nowhere High," he observed, grinning. "Real interesting."

"Yeah, well it was — it is, to me," Darcy insisted. "I kid you not. From the first day . . . it was hard sometimes, but it was worth it. I wasn't a clone, a boarding-school Barbie doll, anymore."

"No, you're not a clone," Josh reflected. "You're different."

"I wanted to fit in, though," Darcy said softly. "With T.J. and Caro. And you."

Josh was silent for a minute. He looked away as if he were embarrassed. *Probably thinking about what a great job I did of fitting in,* Darcy thought. *Alienating people, rather.*

She put out a hand to touch him lightly on the sleeve. "Josh, I don't know how to say it other than the way I've said it already. About that night at Giapetto's, I mean. I'm sorry. I'm just . . . sorry."

"No, Darce, listen." He shoved a shock of dark hair back from his forehead. "I'm the one who's sorry. I wasn't fair to you. I wasn't even going to give you another chance. And that was wrong."

"I don't blame you. I know how I came across," Darcy assured him. "I didn't deal with the situation very well, did I? That credit card thing . . . my family . . . " She hesitated, then forced out the words. "I just found out tonight we're having some financial problems. I didn't know it at the time, though. I was just thrown off balance. It was like getting on a train and then the guy comes around to take your fare and you realize you don't have any money, so he kicks you off while the train's still going a hundred miles an hour."

Josh shook his head. "I don't know why, but I blamed you for that. I mean, obviously you couldn't help it. It wasn't some plot to get me. But I still blamed you."

Now it was Darcy's turn to ask. "Why?"

Hands pushed deep in his pockets, Josh shrugged. "I felt like you were the kind of person who had everything. A BMW, a big house, and an American Express card, you know? It seemed like you had so much that nothing — especially the little subject of our bill — mattered to you."

"It mattered," she said in a small voice. "But I was trying not to show it. You know: when in doubt, act cool."

Josh shrugged. "I guess I felt like I'd been taken for a ride."

Darcy just nodded, her eyes wide and apologetic. Parked, the car had grown cold. She rubbed her small hands together. "Well, I'll take you for a ride now. Got to get the heat on. Where to?"

"How 'bout the burger joint lot?" Josh joked. "Your pal Nick might still be there. . . . "

Darcy grimaced. "Don't even say it! I ever run into him again, I'll die."

"I got an idea." Josh paused as if he were making a decision. "Um, you know Falkowitz's? On Main Street. The art store."

"Sure."

"Well, they had a sign in the window. About a job opening. You know, part-time work."

Josh gave her a funny look, as if he wasn't sure if she *did* know. Darcy laughed. "Yeah, I know what a job is. No kidding, I might need one soon myself."

"Well, obviously they're closed, but maybe we could drive by, see if the help-wanted sign's still up." His face creased in a grin. "Then what d'you say we head back to the station, see if the cops have raided the place yet?"

Smiling, Darcy shifted into gear and drove. *This is better,* she thought, glancing at Josh. *Not cruising, looking for something without knowing what. Going somewhere — this is better.*

Main Street was shut down; a platoon of streetlights cast weak, lemony beams on shuttered storefronts. But to Josh things couldn't have been brighter or clearer if it were high noon.

Stupid to feel so pumped up. It's not like I'm a hero or anything, just 'cause I dished that story to Nick at the station. I did what anybody'd do for a friend.

Darcy cut across the street and braked at the curb. She peered at the art supplies store. "Is that a notice in the window?"

Josh hopped from the car, praying. *I really want this . . .*

A few steps closer and he could read the handwriting on the piece of notebook paper: "Temporary Help Wanted."

"Yaow!" Josh drove a fist into the air, spinning. Darcy was standing on the dark, deserted sidewalk with a smile that took up her whole face. Grabbing her by the waist, Josh lifted her easily, twirling her around until they fell against the BMW, dizzy and laughing.

Josh knew it was ridiculous, but he'd never been so exhilarated. At that instant it seemed to him like anything was possible; he could do anything. Forget school — first thing in the morning, he'd bike over to Falkowitz's and apply for the position.

Darcy was holding him around the waist, still laughing. The indescribable blue of her eyes was the most beautiful color in the world. Rolling with the energy and emotion of the moment, Josh bent down and kissed her. It wasn't a long passionate deal or a split-second peck either, just somewhere nice in between.

"Tell you what, Darcy Jenner." She looked up at him, glowing. "First paycheck from Falkowitz's, if the Witch doesn't steal all of it, we're going back to our restaurant."

She laughed. "Yeah. I owe you."

"No way," Josh said. "Next time we split it."

A minute later, they started on their way to the station. "If you want to just drop me there," Josh suggested, "you can. I know your folks don't like you out late."

Darcy shook her head. "I'm not going home tonight. I suppose tomorrow I'll have to face that scene, but tonight . . . the station will have to be home."

Josh understood. He'd already spent more hours there than he could count. If home was a place where you felt like you could be yourself, then Split River Station *was* his home — his dad's house sure wasn't.

To their surprise, a dim orange glow was creeping through the boarded-up station windows when they arrived. Inside, T.J. and Caroline and Marc were playing poker by the light of the hurricane lamps.

"Great, we could use some more players," T.J. said, by way of a greeting. "Now we're ready for some *strip* poker!"

He and Caro were wedged side by side on the beanbag chair, and she gave him an affectionate cuff on the chin. "Keep dreaming, McAllister," she kidded. Then Josh saw her smile hesitantly at Darcy. "It's okay," Caro said, as if anticipating a remark of Darcy's. "I'm glad you're here."

"I have a long story for you," Darcy promised Caroline, taking a seat next to Marc on the sofa.

"So, when did you guys get here?" Josh asked, knowing it had to be in the past fifteen minutes.

"Just now," Caro answered. "I went by T.J.'s earlier and actually caught him and Marc reading Shakespeare. Can you believe the nerds?"

"She dragged us at gunpoint to her car," Marc added.

"Marc had never had a ride in the Mustang," Caro explained with a grin. "Now his life's complete."

T.J. who'd been twisting a strand of Caro's hair in his fingers, rolled his eyes. Then he grabbed the deck of cards and shuffled with a flourish. "McAllister's Casino Royale and I'm dealing," he declared. "Who's in?"

Everybody was, and T.J. spit the cards around. Marc arranged his with a groan, like he was pretending to have a rotten hand. Josh checked his own hand. It might be a winning one.

"Y'know, I'm starting to like this place," Marc observed as Darcy leaned over the back of the couch to hit the play button on the boombox.

"Just wait till you've lost all your dough to the house," T.J. warned ominously.

Marc laughed. "I'll risk it."

I'll risk it, Josh thought. *I can take risks now, because of these guys, because of Split River Station.* Looking up from his cards, he met Darcy's eyes and he knew that she was thinking the same thing.

If you need someone to talk to . . .

The kids in this book are lucky — when things get rough they can turn to each other. But if you have a problem and there isn't anyone you can talk to, here are some numbers you can call. They're toll free, and someone will be there to help twenty-four hours a day.

Covenant House: 1-800-999-9999
Hit Home Runaway Hotline: 1-800-448-4663
National Child Abuse Hotline: 1-800-422-4453
National Runaway Hotline: 1-800-231-6946
National Runaway Switchboard and Suicide
   Hotline: 1-800-621-4000

If a family member abuses alcohol or you have a problem with cocaine, these numbers can direct you to help in your local area:

Alateen: 1-800-356-9996
1-800-COCAINE or 1-800-262-2463